RUN

WILLIAM SLEATOR

SCHOLASTIC BOOK SERVICES
New York Toronto London Auckland Sydney Tokyo

ISBN 0-590-31767-9

Copyright © 1973 by William Sleator. All rights reserved. This edition is published by Scholastic Book Services, a Division of Scholastic Magazines, Inc., 50 West 44 Street, New York, N.Y. 10036, by arrangement with E. P. Dutton, a Division of Elsevier-Dutton Publishing Co., Inc.

12 11 10 9 8 7 6 5 4 3 2 1   1   1 2 3 4 5 6/8

Printed in the U.S.A.   06

FEAR!

He bent over the bikes, lying against each other on the ground, and the birds wheeled and darted above his head. Why don't they run away? he thought. They should be halfway across the beach by now. Laboriously he dragged the bikes to a standing position. Several birds almost hit him and he felt the continual wind of their passing wings on his arms and head.

Stumbling, he began to steer both bikes toward the road. Their wheels turned toward each other, then away; like living things they struggled to elude his grasp. But soon the gulls were behind him; the cool, comforting sound of the rain began to muffle their cries.

Slowly he made his way up the muddy slope of the road. The dizzying ache in his head had grown worse. But at last the light from the windows drew near. He pushed the bikes across the narrow front lawn, around the side of the house to the back, and left them leaning against the wall by the back door.

Then, as he turned to go inside, he saw a moving shape among the trees. Not a sea gull, something bigger, more like a large animal or even a person. Vague and indistinct, he thought that this *must* be an illusion of the rain, for it vanished quickly. But suddenly he was chilled. Shivering, he hurried into the house.

One

He ran straight for the sea. It was as if something he could not control was pulling him toward the water. He had left his bicycle at the end of the road. Seeing that the beach on the other side of the creek was wide and sandy, he had ripped off his shoes and waded quickly across, dropping them on the other side. Then, his pack bouncing on his back, he began to run.

But whatever was pulling him had no effect on his companion. The other boy stood and watched in dismay as his friend waded into the creek. He had called out to him, he had gestured to him to come back, but he was ignored. Slowly and deliberately the second boy took off his shoes and rolled his jeans up to his knees. He stepped slowly into the water, picking his way carefully across. And then he slipped and fell, soaking his pants. On the other side he stared angrily after his friend, who hadn't noticed, and then sat down and began putting on his shoes.

The phone rang.

Slowly Lillian rose from the lawn, and with blades of new grass clinging to her shorts she walked into the house. It was her mother, of course. Her parents had only been gone for half an hour, and still her mother had to stop at a phone booth and call her, just to make sure that Lillian really felt comfortable about staying by herself overnight.

"Yes, of course I mean it. I already told you ten times. I feel fine."

But her voice sounded more confident than she actually felt. She relished the freedom of being away from her parents for two whole days; relished it enough even to spend the night alone in their isolated summerhouse. It frightened her to think of staying alone, but of course she couldn't let her parents know that, or they would never let her stay. And it was still morning; she didn't have to think about the night yet.

She looked through the kitchen window beside the phone, but the two boys could not be seen from this angle. As her mother talked on, Lillian began running her hand vaguely through her hair. She had only been up for an hour and had not combed it yet. When at last her mother hung up, she dropped the phone carelessly onto the hook and kicked off her sandals, letting them remain where they fell in the middle of the spotless kitchen floor. Her parents didn't approve of going barefoot.

Outside on the lawn again, the boy with black hair, the one who had first crossed the creek, was nowhere to be seen. He must have run off to the other side of the dune, for the other boy, the blond one, was heading in that direction.

Soon he too was out of sight. Lillian waited, but they did not reappear.

She went into the house and ate a candy bar, dropping the wrapper beside the radio on the kitchen counter. She got her brush and comb and a book and went out on the lawn again. For a time she lazily brushed her hair, thinking about nothing, the book lying closed by her side. Soon the dark-haired boy appeared again. His shirt was off and he was running across the top of the dune. He was hardly visible long enough for her to get a good look at him; nor, she realized, had he seemed to notice that the tide was rising. Already the creek had overflowed its banks, and would very soon be too deep to wade across.

She tried to read, but kept glancing up in the direction of the two boys. It was not long before the beach they were on had become an island, the dune like a small mountain in the center. The creek was now a lake, wide and deep.

At last they came around the dune and stood looking toward their inaccessible bikes. The black-haired boy started into the dark rippling water, but soon turned back. It was probably over his head, and in April that water was too cold for anyone to swim through.

Lillian stood up and tossed her long, dark blonde hair back over her shoulders. Still barefoot, she started down the path toward the water.

Two

As she rowed, Lillian kept looking back over her shoulder, not only to check on her direction, but also to see what the boys were doing. At first they didn't notice her. They seemed to be arguing, their opening and closing mouths making no sounds beneath a growing wind from the sea, and the blond one was pacing on the sand. Finally, when she was quite near, she turned her head to find them both looking at her, their hair moving in the wind. She smiled at them, and the blond boy smiled back, with a tentative wave.

She turned again as the boat floated slowly toward them and scraped against the sand. The dark boy, who was taller, was not smiling.

"Well," Lillian said brightly, "it looks as if you got caught."

"Yes," the shorter boy said quickly, stepping closer. "It seemed like this was just a little creek when we first got here."

"There's a very fast tide here. In a few hours it'll be even higher. I guess you've never been here before." Her voice, she noticed, sounded a trifle hoarse above the wind, which made her feel sophisticated. She glanced at the taller boy for a moment, who was still scowling, then back to the other. "So . . . do you want a lift?"

"Of course!" he said, grinning broadly. "We would have had to wait here till we could get to our bikes, and it might have been late by then, and then ride them all wet and cold in the dark."

"Or else . . . stay here," said the dark one softly.

Lillian looked at him again. It was the first thing he had said to her.

"Yes, we might have had to stay here all night. God!" said the other. "I guess we might as well get going." He picked up his knapsack and stepped unsteadily into the boat, which was fiber glass and very light. The dark boy shouldered his pack, put one foot into the boat, and pushed off with the other, stepping lightly inside as they drifted away from shore. The boat wobbled uncertainly as the two of them found their places and sat down. Then Lillian turned the boat around with the oars, rather awkwardly, and began to row.

Crowded together in the stern of the tiny boat, the two boys watched the opposite bank as they approached it, avoiding her eyes. Suddenly the blond one leaned forward. "Is that where you live?" he almost whispered. "It looks so *haunted*."

Why, it does look haunted, Lillian thought, turning toward it. The house seemed different, as if she were seeing it for the first time. The unpainted wooden shingles gave it a look of age and disrepair, as though no one had lived there for years, and the sagging, sharply pitched roofs of its different wings rose up into the sky at odd, disparate angles. Situated at the top of the hill, the house almost seemed to be floating as the clouds sailed past behind, held to earth only by the bare trees surrounding it, groping at the house with twisted fingers.

In the dark kitchen window, Lillian suddenly thought she saw a moving light. She blinked, and the light was gone. She took a deep breath. Stop it, she said to herself. Stop imagining things and making it worse.

She turned back to the boys, trying to laugh. "My mother vacuums all the ghosts away," she said. But my mother will be gone tonight, she remembered. I'm going to be all alone there.

As they moved toward the house, bobbing gently in the boat, the house seemed to rise up and lean over them. Behind it and to the right the trees grew more thickly together, becoming a small wood. Already the darkness between the trees was too thick to see through, so that the woods appeared dense and impenetrable. The branches were beginning to move slightly, rustling. There was no other house in sight.

The boat came to rest beneath a tree and they stepped out. Lillian looked briefly at the woods again, turning quickly away from the sight of all those gray, creaking branches and the blackness behind them. The wind was cold on her neck now, lifting the strands of her hair. She shivered. And then the thought occurred to her: perhaps she didn't have to stay alone in the house tonight after all.

"Would you like to come in for a minute?" she said. "It's really getting chilly, you might like to get warmed up before you go."

"Great," the blond one said. "It is getting cold."

"But what about getting to the hostel?" the other one asked.

"Oh, we'll make it," the blond boy said, dismissing his friend's statement with a wave of his hand. "You know it's close. We were just going to ride around all day anyway."

"Where are you going?" asked Lillian.

"Well, see, we're on a bike trip. We left home this morning and we're going to stay in a hostel tonight and then end up at a friend's tomorrow night. But I'm sure we still have time. Come on."

"My name is Lillian," she said, as the two of them started up the hill.

"I'm Jerry, and that's Mark," said the blond boy, pointing at his friend, who had remained standing by the boat, staring back at the island.

Lillian turned to look at him, wondering why he wasn't coming with them; but she quickly brought her eyes back to the ground to watch for stones that would bite into her still tender feet, hopping slightly to avoid them. They were on a narrow path that wound up the hill through the trees and tangled underbrush toward a perfect lawn at the back of the house.

"Will your parents mind if we just drop in like this?" Jerry asked her.

"How can they? They're not even here," she said. "They had to go back to New York, and they won't be back till late tomorrow night. They wanted me to go with them, but I wouldn't. Why should I waste part of spring vacation in the city, with them?"

"You shouldn't, of course."

She glanced back at Mark again, who had begun to make his own way up the hill through the trees. "Your friend," she whispered. "Is there anything . . . funny about him?"

"Funny? No. Why do you ask?"

"Oh, I don't know, he just seemed so quiet, and sort of brooding. He's hardly said two words to me yet. He acts as if he hates me."

"No, no," Jerry said, shaking his head for emphasis. "It's just his way. He doesn't hate you." But he turned back to look at Mark and an apprehensive look flashed across his face, as though he wasn't absolutely sure about what he was saying. "He never talks much, not even to me."

On the lawn they stopped to wait for Mark, watching him thread his way between the trees. He managed a brief smile as he approached them, and Jerry, standing beside her, seemed to relax.

"It's nice here," Mark said, joining them and turning to look at the view. "You can see the marsh and the sea and everything."

"Do you like the sea?" Lillian asked, watching his round, rather pimply face, trying to see what was hidden behind his guarded expression.

"Yes, I like the sea," he said quietly.

"Come on, let's go inside," Jerry said. "I want to see what this haunted house is like."

I wish he'd stop saying that, thought Lillian. The wind was stronger now, all around them the trees were sighing, and she shivered again. The house would not be very warm tonight, she realized, and it would be big, and dark, and it would creak. She started walking toward it, wishing that her parents had painted it some bright color instead of leaving those dark gray shingles all over it. And then she saw that the door was wide open, swinging back and forth in the breeze.

"Hey!" she said, and stopped. A cold finger ran up her back. It was the way the door was moving, as though something were pushing it, beckoning her into the darkness inside.

"What's the matter?" said Jerry.

"The door's open."

"So what?"

"But I always close it, I never leave it open." Her parents had told her so many times to close doors behind her that it was now an automatic response.

"How can you be so sure?" He was looking at her strangely, as though afraid something had gone wrong. "People always forget to close doors, don't they?"

"But — well, yes, I guess so," she murmured, telling herself not to be so silly and starting forward again.

Just inside the back door was a small entryway, and then the kitchen, brand-new, gleaming and green, its perfect order marred only by the sandals and candy wrapper she had dropped. Jerry looked slightly disappointed, as though he had expected thick dust and spiderwebs.

"And this is the cozy room," Lillian announced as she led them through a doorway on the right. Both boys' eyes moved at once to the dominant feature of the room.

"Is this a real ship's lantern?" Jerry asked,

touching the glass of a large, shiny brass lantern which hung from a heavy chain over a polished wooden table.

"Be careful," Lillian said quickly. "Please don't get finger marks on it. Yes, it is a real ship's lantern. It's my parents' pride and joy. They're always getting things in ship supply stores and putting them all over the house, even though all they have is that little rowboat. I guess it's kind of ridiculous."

"Cozy room?" Jerry asked, his gaze wandering to the rest of the room, which contained nothing but four fragile maple colonial chairs and a fireplace. Over most of the middle of the floor was a thin hooked rug.

"This is where we spend most of our time," Lillian explained. But why does it seem so dark in here? she wondered, looking past Jerry to the window. The sky was heavily overcast, only a few pale shafts of light breaking through to illuminate a swaying tree or a patch of dark water. She could hear the wind shaking the attic window, and suddenly a door slammed upstairs, and she flinched. All at once she remembered how isolated she always felt in her small bed at night, far from where her parents slept; how the house seemed to breathe through all the dark empty rooms above and below her; how the endless blackness outside pressed against the lonely building, creeping in through the windows, full of unfamiliar rustling sounds. She knew she wouldn't sleep tonight, and she imagined herself lying there awake, fearful in the darkness, listening. Listening, perhaps, for the door to open again. . . .

No, she said to herself, don't think that way. But she couldn't help it; the thoughts kept coming back. She looked quickly at Jerry, then to Mark. There was obviously nothing to be afraid of in them. If only she could get them to stay! But how can I do it? she was asking herself, when with a suddenness and violence that made her start, it began to rain.

Mark hurried to the window. The wind was blowing with such force that the rain beat almost horizontally against the glass with a harsh, rattling sound. "The bikes!" he said. "We've got to get them inside!"

"I'm not going out there. It sounds like it's hailing," said Jerry.

"You certainly couldn't bring them in here. They'll be all wet and muddy," Lillian said.

"But . . . we've got to do *something* with them!" Mark was almost shouting. "They'll rust."

"Well, *I* don't care if you bring them in, but my parents can't stand any dirt in the house, and it would be a big mess to clean up."

"But we should at least get them into the yard." He turned to Jerry.

"I'm not going out there," Jerry insisted. "You can go get yours if you want, but I don't see what difference it would make. They're going to get wet anyway, and no one would be out there stealing them in the rain."

"Can't you just wipe them off when it stops raining?"

"Oh, all right." Mark took a few quick steps away from the window, then back, beating his fist against his palm. "But . . . but now what are we going to do? I guess we can't leave for a while."

"It's so lucky we came in," Jerry said. "We'd be out there in the rain now if we hadn't."

To Lillian, it was the storm that was lucky. Even though its suddenness was rather unnerving it couldn't have been more perfect if she'd made it happen herself. She only hoped the rain would last long enough to make it impossible for them to get to the hostel. But she couldn't depend on that; she had to keep them interested enough so that even if it did stop raining they wouldn't think of leaving until it was too late. Jerry, she thought, would be no problem; he seemed to want to stay. Mark was the tough one. He behaved as though he hated being inside, as though her presence made him nervous, and she found herself resenting him slightly. She had to think of something to make him forget about going outside.

"I know what we can do," she said. "Did you guys eat yet? We could have lunch."

"Good idea," Jerry said. "We didn't eat and I'm starving."

"But what about . . . we were going to have a picnic," said Mark.

"I know, Mark," Jerry said. "I really wanted one too. But in the rain?" He sighed. "Look, I don't understand the problem. We know the hostel isn't very far, the whole point was to take it easy and explore a little bit." He turned to Lillian. "That's why we came down this road. It's not on the way. So since it's raining anyway, we might as well stay here till it stops. We have plenty of time. Let's just forget about it and enjoy ourselves for a while. Isn't it true that storms like this never last very long?"

"Not necessarily," Mark said gloomily.

What's eating him? Lillian wondered. This could be fun. What is there to dislike about it?

"Well anyway," Jerry said, "we'll ride better after we've eaten."

"Good," said Lillian, moving toward the kitchen. "Then it's settled?"

"I guess so," said Mark, and turned away.

Three

Lillian planned as she searched the kitchen shelves. There was food her mother had prepared before leaving, but that should be saved for — hopefully — dinner for three. But she had to find something good *now*, something better than what they might get at a hostel. There were some mysterious foil-wrapped packages in the freezer compartment of the refrigerator, but it would take too long to thaw them, so from the shelves she culled what she had to admit were rather ordinary things: cheese, bread, canned soup, and tuna fish.

Jerry, it turned out, liked to cook. "Grilled cheese sandwiches!" he said. "I love them."

"But do you know how to make them?"

"No, but I'm sure we can figure it out. The first thing is to cut off some slices of cheese, I guess."

Which they proceeded to do. While they worked, Lillian was longing to ask Jerry more about Mark. Jerry seemed so open and friendly, especially in contrast to Mark's sullenness, and she couldn't figure out why they were friends. Also, the more she knew about Mark, the better able she would be to get him to stay overnight. But she had to restrain her curiosity. Mark, standing by the window in the other room, might hear them. And Jerry seemed to have a certain loyalty to him which she did not yet feel ready to test.

So she talked about her parents. "They never leave me alone," she said, as the slice of cheese she was cutting crumbled in half. (Jerry's slices were all thin and perfect.) "They're always after me to comb my hair, put on my shoes, blah blah blah. I still can't believe they let me stay here by myself overnight." She glanced at his face, hoping he would say, "Overnight, all by yourself? But are you sure it's safe? Shouldn't we stay?" But he didn't, of course. "And when they come back, I know they'll check into every nook and cranny to be sure the house is in perfect shape. But I'm so glad they let me stay. There's *so* much to do here, even in the rain." It was easy to talk to him, because he seemed attentive and interested, even while concentrating on the cheese.

"Good," he said. "Although I hope the rain doesn't last too long. The hostel has a curfew. And also Mark — both of us — " he added quickly, "were planning to do some exploring."

"Oh, there's lots to see around here," Lillian said hastily. "I could show you some good places, if the rain stops."

Like what? she asked herself, her mind racing over all the local scenic spots, and coming up with nothing she felt would interest them.

"Oh, good," he said vaguely. "If we have time. Now I guess we should put the cheese on the bread."

"How are you going to cook them?"

"Just like they do in a drugstore. Melt butter in the pan, fry them, and push down on them with a pancake turner."

Lillian watched him as he leaned, fascinated, over the three sandwiches sputtering in the pan. His long, pale hair hung down over his checks, his blue eyes, set close together in a narrow, rather pretty face, gazed raptly at the toasting bread. But his interest in what he was doing didn't interfere with their conversation in the least, and in a few minutes they were laughing together quite naturally.

"The elevator was real crowded," Jerry was saying, "and my sister was sucking her thumb, and this old lady said, 'Now you mustn't suck your thumb, little girl,' so my sister took her thumb out of her mouth, and mother glared at the old lady and said to my sister, 'Put your thumb *back* in your mouth!' "

"How wonderful!" Lillian cried, clapping her hands. "Your mother sounds so different from mine!"

She turned at the sound of a footstep to see Mark standing in the doorway, staring at them balefully. Jerry looked at him, smiled nervously, then turned back to the pan. "Does the rain . . . seem to be stopping?" he said. In an instant, the atmosphere in the room had changed completely.

"No," Mark said in his expressionless voice. "Is there a radio or anything? There might be a weather report."

So what? thought Lillian. Whether you know or not, you still can't go until it stops. His quite obvious impatience to leave was beginning to irritate her. "Right behind you on the counter, beside the window," she said.

Mark turned. "Where?"

"Right *there*, where you — hey!" she said suddenly, hurrying across the room. "It's not there."

"Is that where it's supposed to be?" Jerry asked, turning the sandwiches over.

"Yes." She frowned at the empty counter. "I thought I just saw it there. What could have happened to it?" She knew that her parents had probably just moved it, but suddenly another idea occurred to her. If she could make the boys think she was in some kind of danger, then they would have to stay. "Do you think it could be . . . *stolen?*" she said.

"Oh, of course not," said Jerry. "Who would come all the way out here to steal a radio? I bet somebody just moved it."

"Maybe. . . ." she said doubtfully. She turned to Mark. "That means if you still want to hear it, I have to go look all over the whole house, I guess."

Sighing, she glared at him. He stared impassively back at her. She waited for him to offer to help, and when he didn't she flounced out of the room, letting the door slam behind her. The rest of the house was cold and dark, and as she hurried through the sparsely furnished rooms her irritation grew. Even if she found it, she decided, she would tell them she hadn't, just so they might possibly think it had been stolen. And it would please her to prevent Mark from hearing the weather report. But she didn't find it.

Mark's angry voice and Jerry's placating one were coming through the kitchen door as she returned. She did not hesitate, but plunged into the room, to be greeted by that charged silence that means one's presence has stopped a conversation dead.

"It's nowhere," she said. "I looked all over the house and it's nowhere. I bet it *has* been stolen."

Jerry and Mark seemed to be too involved in whatever they had been talking about to pay much attention to the radio. Jerry, still fiddling with the sandwiches, looked miserable; Mark's cheeks were glowing and his small mouth had a tight, pinched look.

"Well," Jerry said, sounding as though it were a tremendous effort to think about her trivial problem, "are you sure it was here at all? Maybe your parents took it with them to get it fixed or something."

"But. . . ." Lillian tried to concentrate. She hadn't believed it really might be stolen when she had first said it, but now she was beginning to wonder. *Had* she seen it after her parents left? She couldn't remember. "Well, maybe. I'll ask them if they call again. They probably will. But it still might be stolen." She turned to Mark. "You'll have to try to get the news on TV. That's in the living room." Mark left the kitchen without a word.

In a moment they heard the television go on, and under the cover of its squawking and bleating, Jerry said softly, "I'm sorry Mark seems so . . . funny, and that he didn't help you look for the radio. He's just sort of shy, and he was really looking forward to riding around all day out here. He's really okay, basically."

"Mmmm," said Lillian. But you're so nice, she felt like saying, and he's so creepy. How come you're his friend? She sniffed at the air. "Hey!" she said, "What's that smell?"

"Oh, no!" Jerry cried, spinning around to the smoking sandwiches. But it was too late. He could barely get their blackened remains out of the pan.

Four

Lunch did not turn out quite the way Lillian had hoped. All that could be salvaged of the sandwiches were single slices of greasy bread with gummy bits of cheese clinging to them. She started making tuna-fish salad without realizing that there was no more mayonnaise; so she used bottled Roquefort dressing instead, with doubtful results. Even the tomato soup was watery (she was saving the milk for breakfast, just in case), and full of lumps.

Oh well, she said to herself, watching them pick at the meal, food would never have gotten them to stay anyway. The one thing that will keep them here is having fun. The only trouble with that idea was that Lillian herself was in no mood for fun. The failure of the meal had depressed her; the rain, to her annoyance, seemed to be slackening; Mark's silent presence got on her nerves; and she did not have the ability to be charming and create a good time when she wasn't in the right mood.

Jerry, it seemed, did. It was not long before he

began making jokes, friendly ones, about the food. He described other disastrous meals he had had, which led Lillian to mention some herself, and even Mark told a story about his mother putting garlic powder in a cake instead of salt. By the time they finished (none of them ate much), they almost *were* having fun. Lillian kept looking out at the rain, unable to tell if it really was letting up or if she were just imagining it, and then to the clock. As it moved past two o'clock she began silently urging it on. The later it got, after all, the less chance they'd have of getting to the hostel before it closed; she had to keep them here until then.

For now she was more apprehensive than ever about being alone at night. Added to her growing awareness of how big and dark the house would seem was her worry about the radio. It was probably silly of her, Jerry was probably right, but she knew that once she was alone she would not be able to forget about it. Maybe she should just come right out and ask them to stay, tell them she was afraid. But how timid she would seem, not independent at all; they would think it was babyish of her. No, she would only do that as a last resort.

"A big plastic bubble," Jerry was saying, "sort of like those amoeba things we looked at in science class. Her father likes to swim a million laps every day and they put it over the pool so he could swim even in winter. It's real eerie inside, all steamy and everything, you can hardly see across the pool."

"I was thinking . . . I was thinking we might be able to swim on this trip," Mark said.

"In *April?*" said Lillian.

"Oh, Mark's a nature boy," Jerry said. "He likes things like swimming in cold water and taking long hikes and stuff."

"Do you?" she asked.

"Oh, sure, of course." But he didn't sound as though he meant it. He often seemed to say things he didn't really mean, Lillian was beginning to notice.

"And I like riding bikes too," Mark said. He was looking out the window. "If only it wasn't raining quite so hard, we could be out there riding right now. I wouldn't mind getting a little bit wet."

"But our clothes," Jerry said. "They'd get soaked and we don't have any others. It would be freezing and horrible."

"Well, if it doesn't stop pretty soon we're going to have to do it anyway." He looked at the clock. "I know the hostel isn't very far, but it'll be slow going, and they don't let you in after the curfew."

"Oh, I'm sure it'll stop pretty soon," Lillian said quickly. "You might as well wait till it stops. We can . . . um . . . we can play . . Monopoly!" She tried to say the word as though it were the most thrilling activity in the world "I just love Monopoly, it's so much fun."

"Monopoly!" Mark said with disgust. "You mean monotony. Isn't that what you always call it, Jerry?"

"Do I?" Jerry said, looking uncomfortable. "But that was just a joke. It's not really a bad game. Do you want to play?" he asked her.

Lillian herself loathed Monopoly. "Yes!" she said fervently. "Everybody always has fun when we play. It's right over here in the closet." She jumped up. But the game wasn't there; and she suddenly remembered with a sinking feeling how she had thrown it into the ocean last summer after a particularly painful weekend of it with her parents. "Oh, but I know!" she went on, picking up another game. "If you don't like Monopoly, Mark, we can play this." She sat down and began laying out the board and pieces. "It's really a much better game. I just forgot about it. It's a detective game, and the point is to figure out who did the murder."

Jerry was frankly interested; and though Mark only grudgingly consented to play, after about half an hour even he began to get involved. Lillian, it turned out, was the only one who didn't enjoy it. Every time you made a move it was necessary to say something like, "I suggest that Mr. Prune killed him in the ballroom with a carving knife," or "Miss Pineapple did it in the conservatory with a poker." It was getting quite dark out now, and Lillian's mind kept straying to the real poker by the fireplace, the real carving knife in the kitchen, and her own helpless self huddled upstairs in bed. She lost miserably.

By the time they were finishing the third game it was almost impossible to see the board. Lillian had avoided turning on the light for fear of reminding them that it was getting late. But naturally Mark was the first one to notice the time.

"Hey!" he said, "it's after four-thirty. And it's so dark out, pretty soon we won't be able to see at all." He stood up. "Come on, Jerry, we've really got to get going."

"But it's still raining," Lillian said. "Hear it? It sounds like it's raining terribly hard."

Jerry was obviously torn. He looked out the window nervously, then back to the clock. But at last he made the decision. "I guess we really should," he said, and slowly stood up.

It was Lillian's last chance. She took a deep breath. "You could always . . . you could stay here overnight, if you didn't want to get wet. My parents won't be back till tomorrow."

"That's nice of you," Jerry said, brightening a bit. He looked at Mark. "But. . . ."

Mark seemed to be annoyed by the invitation. "But then we'll have to ride so far tomorrow."

"Not that far," said Jerry. "You know we could make it."

"But we wouldn't have much time to explore, then. And I'm tired of just sitting around here, I've got to get outside. I don't care if it is raining."

"We could have a really good dinner," Lillian said frantically. "My mother made it last night. She's a wonderful cook. And, we could . . . we could . . ." Then it hit her. "We could have *wine*. There's an open bottle, they'll never miss it. Did you ever have wine before?"

"No," said Jerry. "I've always wondered what it was like."

"Maybe you could just eat here," Lillian said. If she could only keep them here a little longer, maybe then she could convince them to stay all night. "You'll probably miss dinner at the hostel anyway, and if you have to ride in the rain, you'll feel better if you've eaten something hot. And it's already completely dark out, so it won't be any easier to see now than later." It was so dark in the room that she could barely see their faces. "What time does the hostel close, anyway?"

"Ten-thirty," Jerry said. "How long will it take to get there, Mark?"

"An hour and a half, at least."

"But then we have plenty of time," Jerry said, sounding relieved. "And I'm starving. I didn't eat much for lunch. And it might stop raining after dinner."

Lillian waited tensely as Mark looked back and forth between her and Jerry. "Oh, all right," he said at last. "Let's stay for dinner. But we better eat pretty soon. It might take longer than we think to get to the hostel."

"Oh, sure," Lillian said, beaming at him, suddenly feeling immensely grateful. Now she wanted to be as nice to him as possible. "We'll eat right away. And if you want to watch the weather report, you can bring the TV in here where it's warm."

"Maybe I'll do that," Mark said gruffly, and quickly left the room.

Lillian turned to Jerry. They were both smiling, and it seemed to her that he shared her feeling of relief, the same wonderful feeling she had when school was let out for the summer. Now she was sure she could get them to stay overnight.

Chattering gaily, the two of them went into the kitchen. Mark watched the weather report alone, in the dark.

Five

By the time they sat down to eat, the rain had diminished to a barely perceptible drizzle.

For a short time Lillian had stopped worrying altogether as she bustled about in the kitchen, warming the food, tearing up lettuce, giggling over Jerry's stories. No one had bothered to turn on the light in the cozy room, and when she entered with plates and silverware she could see through the window, where Mark was standing again, that the sky was almost clear behind the twisted shapes of the trees. There were only a few scattered splashes on the windowpane, and, her anxiety flowing back, she slammed the dishes onto the table and switched on the ship's lantern, thereby extinguishing the view and filling the room with a harsh glare that penetrated coldly into every corner.

"God, it's cold in here," Jerry said as soon as they sat down.

"I'll turn up the heat," said Lillian, moving to the thermostat on the wall.

"Maybe we could build a fire," said Mark.

Lillian paused, standing behind her chair. Fires were such a mess, her parents hardly ever had them, it would just mean more cleaning up for her later. On the other hand, she would do almost anything to get Mark and Jerry to stay. But she had to stretch things out. Decisively, she sat down.

"Sure," she said. "But let's have it later. The food will get cold if we do it now."

"What is this?" Jerry asked.

"Oh, it's a thing my mother makes. It has chicken and spaghetti in it, and cornflakes and cheese on top. Help yourself."

She watched Jerry rather hesitantly dip his spoon into her mother's favorite pastel blue casserole dish, wondering for the first time how old he was. Her gaze moved to Mark as he served himself. His black hair was unfashionably short (Jerry's fell well below his ears), but there was something sullen and rebellious in his expression that kept him from looking boring, as she usually assumed anyone with short hair to be.

"Hey!" she said, "we forgot about the wine!" As she hurried into the kitchen her good spirits returned at the thought of doing something so forbidden, and reputedly so pleasurable.

"Are you sure your parents won't mind?" Jerry said.

She was already pouring the wine into three glasses. "They'll never know, so what difference does it make?"

The wine was unpleasantly sour, but Lillian gulped down most of her glass, closing her eyes and holding her breath so as not to taste it.

"Well!" she said, pouring more wine without waiting for them to ask for it, "there's really a lot left."

"This food," Jerry said politely, "It's . . . good."

"Is it?" Lillian said, pushing cornflakes over to the side of her plate. "I don't like the cornflakes, but my mother says that's what gives the dish its *Je ne sais quoi*. Do you like it, Mark?"

"You know me," Mark said to Jerry. Suddenly he seemed to be smiling more often than usual, Lillian noticed. "I hardly know what I'm eating. It tastes all right. I'm hungry."

"My mother loves to cook," said Lillian, "but it never interested me. Not that she'd ever let me get close enough to the stove to learn how. I make too much of a mess." She took a big drink from her glass, forgetting that it was wine, and only barely managed to cover up her reaction to the sudden stinging taste. There was nothing else to drink on the table, and all three of them were using the wine to wash down their food.

"How old are you guys, anyway?" Lillian asked.

"I'm fourteen," Jerry said, "And Mark's almost fifteen."

"Oh, really. I *am* fifteen," said Lillian.

"So you're an 'older woman,'" Jerry said, looking at her as though she were more interesting with this revelation.

"Yesss . . ." she leaned forward. "And I do things like drink." She took a sip of wine. Ugh, she thought, how can anyone stand this stuff? Although she was beginning to feel strangely light and silly, she noticed. "Come on, drink your wine, you guys!" she said. "Your glasses are still almost full."

"I don't like it," said Mark.

"Neither do I," said Lillian. "In fact, I can hardly stand it. But it's supposed to make you feel good, so we might as well drink it while we have the chance."

"But not as good as . . . other things," Jerry said mysteriously.

"Oh, of course," she said quickly. She couldn't let him think she was out of it. "Do you guys turn on?"

"Yes!" Jerry said quickly. "I mean, I've tried it. Mark hasn't."

"Why not?" Lillian asked.

"I don't know," Mark said reluctantly. "I was just never interested.

"Oh," she said. As far as she knew, there wasn't any marijuana around her school, and she had never tried it herself. But she certainly wasn't going to tell them. She turned to Jerry. "I don't suppose you happen to have any with you."

"No."

"Too bad. It would have been so much fun to have some here with my parents away and all." She sighed tragically and took another sip of wine. There was a brief silence. Jerry finished his wine; and Mark, as if he were trying to find something to do with his hands, drained his glass well.

"Well, at last you've finished," Lillian said. "Here, have some more." She rose unsteadily to pour, but Mark covered his glass with his hand. "Oh, come on," she said.

"No, really."

"Well, you'll have a teentsy bit more, then," she said to Jerry, and poured some into his glass. "And I'll just have a teentsy bit more," and poured some into her glass. "And then I'll put the rest away for —" Reaching for the cork, she set the bottle down on the edge of her plate and it toppled over onto the table too quickly for anyone to grab it. "Oh dearie me!" she cried wittily as the wine flowed out over the wood and onto the rug. Mark jumped up and set the bottle upright, but all the wine had been lost. "Oh, what a waste!" Lillian giggled as she sank into her chair. "I suppose we'll have to clean it up sometime. But not now, I feel too good." She sighed happily and took another sip. She didn't notice the taste so much anymore, so it was easier to drink. "If only my parents could see me now! Sitting here drinking wine with two boys I don't even know. . . ."

"Well, you know something about us," Jerry said. "But what you *don't* know is that at midnight, we turn into two blooooodthirsty vampires —"

Lillian tried not to giggle, but she couldn't help it. He was so funny, the way he suddenly narrowed his eyes and began to smile crookedly.

" — who will creep into your bedroom and sink our fangs into the tender flesh of your neck —" His voice dropped, " — and then we will drink the living blood from your veins until you are nothing but a pile of skin and bones. . . ." And suddenly he bared his teeth, snarled, and leapt toward her.

Lillian shrieked. For an instant she jumped up;

then both of them collapsed back into their chairs.

When she raised her head from the table she realized that Mark hadn't even been laughing, just staring dully down at his plate. But it was the funniest thing in the world, how could he not laugh? She was still dimly conscious of the need to keep him entertained, however, and noticed that his plate was empty. She pushed herself to her feet.

"Does anybody want some dessert?" she said. "Well, I do."

She wandered into the kitchen, pausing in the doorway to steady herself. Things kept getting in her way. She opened the refrigerator door, stumbling as she leaned against it. She knew there was something in here, but what? Her eyes explored the shelves. Was it — and she slumped against the door again, laughing quietly — was it that marshmallow stuff her mother had made? She mustn't forget to tell them about that. But there was something else. Oh yes, ice cream. She pulled the carton out of the freezer and reached for a white bowl on a lower shelf. But finding she couldn't handle both at once, she set the ice cream down on the counter and stumbled back into the other room with the bowl.

"Here's dessert!" she sang out, sinking into her chair and laughing uncontrollably. She thrust the white bowl at Jerry. It was filled with a solid white mass. Jerry touched it gingerly, and it sprang quickly back.

"What is this?" he said. "Some kind of . . . pudding?"

"Taste it . . . taste it," she managed to gasp, still laughing.

Smiling, Jerry reached in and began to pull some of it out. Like rubber, it stretched and stretched, then suddenly broke. He licked it.

"Hmmm," he said. "It tastes like . . . marshmallows."

"No, not marshmallows!" Lillian cried. "It is *a* marshmallow. One marshmallow. My mother was trying to make homemade marshmallows —" She looked up. Jerry was laughing again, and even Mark. "And, and she put in too much gelatine, and it hardened into this one, huge marshmallow. And there it is. Solid as a rock. The biggest marshmallow in the world!"

Jerry was beating the table with his fists. "I can't stand it!" he moaned. Lillian was rolling back in her chair. "Oh," she sighed, "Oh. . . ."

After a while she noticed that no one was laughing anymore, and she looked up. Both boys were yawning. She pushed herself up on the arms of the chair. "Doesn't anybody want a slice of marshmallow?" she said.

"Er . . . no thanks," said Jerry. Mark didn't bother to say anything.

"Neither do I," she said. "I'm too tired to eat; too tired to laugh anymore."

Jerry was resting his head on his arms, crossed before him on the table. His eyes were closed. "So am I," he said. "All I can say is, sleep is so wonderful."

"The hostel," Mark tried to say, but a yawn interrupted him. "Shouldn't we . . . oh, I don't know. . . ." His chin fell against his chest.

34

"Hey," Lillian said hoarsely. "What's happening?" Without moving, they both opened their eyes, then closed them at once, not answering her. Lillian found that she had to close one eye to focus; with both opened there were two of everything. It was disturbing, in a vague kind of way, and so much easier to leave the eye closed.

"Hey!" she said again, looking at them with one eye. This time they paid no attention at all. Why wouldn't they listen to her? How boring of them to fall asleep! She wanted to wake them up, but it was too much trouble to move from her chair. Very slowly, the whole world seemed to be tilting steadily to the right. She didn't like that. It was much better when she closed the other eye too.

She let her head sink down onto the table, too exhausted to remember the open door or the missing radio or what they might mean; too exhausted to be afraid.

Six

Sudden and chilling, like the blade of a knife, a shriek cut through the steady murmur of the rain.

Mark lifted his head. He opened his eyes, then closed them at once. The image of Lillian, Jerry, and the dirty dishes sprawled across the table under the glaring light faded behind his eyelids.

Outside, the shrieking went on and on.

He shook his head. It felt as though it was full of thick syrup, and there was a pounding in his temples. What on earth was going on out there? And the bikes! It must have started raining again. They were still out by the edge of the water. The tides were strange here. . . . A vivid picture of waves washing over the bicycles and dragging them out to sea suddenly filled his mind.

He pushed himself, lurching, to his feet. He felt a wave of nausea as he focused on the dry, crusted noodles in the casserole, on that sodden mass of marshmallow. The floor was sticky with spilled wine, pulling at his feet as he started to move. He had to get outside, into the rain, to the bikes, to whatever was happening there.

For a moment all he could see were the two patches of light from the windows stretched across the lawn. The sky and the trees were invisible in the darkness that seemed a solid thing all around him — a living thing of gusty sound that welcomed him with chill fingers.

He turned toward the sea, where there was a glow over the horizon and an occasional glimpse of flying foam. The sound of the rain was near his ears, brittle against wood and leaves; the creaking of the trees was farther away, and behind it the ocean was a dull roar. But above them all were the cries he had heard from inside, suddenly distant, suddenly frighteningly close.

And all at once they were familiar. As his eyes adjusted, trees, the hillside, the path began slowly to emerge, blurred through sheets of water. The path was muddy; he found himself grabbing at slippery trees and stumbling into the underbrush as he started down.

The lake, he began to see, had become a creek again; the shrieks seemed to be coming from where the creek emptied into the sea. "That's just where the bikes are," he said softly. He stepped out from beneath the trees, and his feet sank into the spongy turf of the marsh. It was difficult to see, for the water kept getting into his eyes. His clothes were wet through. But he kept going, toward the bikes, for even though he knew it was low tide he could not rid himself of the thought that they might be swept out to sea.

At first the white shapes seemed to be a trick of the rain, fading and reappearing as they darted through the thick darkness. They grew clearer as he neared the sea, and at last, in the very midst of them, he saw the bicycles.

He paused. Sea gulls were familiar to him. But these gulls were different. Their movements were aggressive, not soaring or free, and there was madness in their cries.

Carefully he stepped closer. He was determined, now more than ever, to get the bikes. A few of the birds darted away as he approached, but the nearer he came to the center of them, the more they ignored him. He was almost stepping on them as they hopped away from his feet. Their cries rang painfully in his ears, all but obliterating the sounds of the sea and the rain.

He bent over the bikes, lying against each other on the ground, and the birds wheeled and darted above his head. Why don't they run away? he thought. They should be halfway across the beach by now. Laboriously he dragged the bikes to a standing position. Several birds almost hit him and he felt the continual wind of their passing wings on his arms and head.

Stumbling, he began to steer both bikes toward the road. Their wheels turned toward each other, then away; like living things they struggled to elude his grasp. But soon the gulls were behind him; the cool, comforting sound of the rain began to muffle their cries.

Slowly he made his way up the muddy slope of the road. The dizzying ache in his head had grown worse. But at last the light from the windows drew near. He pushed the bikes across the narrow front lawn, around the side of the house to the back, and left them leaning against the wall by the back door.

Then, as he turned to go inside, he saw a moving shape among the trees. Not a sea gull, something bigger, more like a large animal or even a person. Vague and indistinct, he thought that this *must* be an illusion of the rain, for it vanished quickly. But suddenly he was chilled. Shivering, he hurried into the house.

Jerry and Lillian had not moved. Exhausted and confused, he slumped into his chair and dropped his head onto the sticky tabletop.

Seven

For what seemed like hours Lillian tried to ignore the hard surface beneath her head, that horrible taste and dryness in her mouth, so that she could just go back to sleep. But the discomfort grew worse instead of going away, and at last she was forced to open her eyes and slowly lift her head.

The room was dreary and colorless in the gray morning light. She sighed, trying to push down a growing nausea. Her eyes fell on the spilled wine on the table and a sharp memory of its taste came to her mouth. She almost gagged.

The sight of Jerry and Mark still peacefully asleep filled her with resentment. It wasn't fair that she should be awake in this mess, feeling rotten, while they were oblivious to it all. She had never felt so cranky and irritable. "Hey!" she said, "wake up."

There was no response. She reached over and shook Jerry's shoulder. "Wake up!" she said again, her voice rasping in her dry throat.

Jerry opened his eyes for an instant. "Wha . . .?" he mumbled, and turned his head over.

Lillian was incensed. How could he ignore her like that? "Come on, wake up," she said loudly.

Mark raised his head and looked at her blearily. "Oh, can't you please shut up," he said. "I'm trying to sleep."

"So am I trying to sleep," she said, "but I can't. It's morning. How can you just go on sleeping in that uncomfortable way?"

"You didn't seem to have much trouble last night," he said, putting his head back on the table.

"Well, I can't sleep anymore," said Lillian. She shook her head, pushed her hair out of her eyes, and looked around her. She shuddered visibly. "Yich, what a mess! We're going to have to do something about it. And I feel so sick!"

"So do I," said Jerry, lifting his head at last. "It must have been the wine."

"Ugh! Don't *mention* it!" she said. "The thought of it makes me want to puke." She sighed and sank against the back of the chair. "Hey," she said hoarsely, and cleared her throat, "hey, Mark, what's that puddle next to your head?"

"What?" Mark raised his head again. "Puddle . . . ?"

"There's a puddle of water there," said Jerry, "right where you were sleeping."

Mark rubbed his eyes and looked down at the table. "Oh," he said. "Water. Oh, yeah. I went outside last night."

"In the pouring rain?" Lillian said. "Why?"

Somehow the fact that Mark had gone outside irritated her all the more.

"To get the bikes. I kept thinking they were going to get washed away."

"But that's ridiculous," said Lillian. "They were perfectly safe at high tide, and the tide must have been low then."

"I know." He rubbed his eyes again. "But . . . I just kept having this picture in my mind of the bikes being washed away. Also I felt sick. So I went out there. It was like a nightmare."

"Why?" Jerry asked.

"It was strange. It seems like a dream now. A lot of shrieking woke me up. I had no idea what was making it. And then I went down to the water, and there was a swarm of sea gulls, right at the mouth of the creek where the bikes were. They were flying around and screaming and acting crazy, and they didn't even fly very far away from me."

"Yes," Lillian said, "they do that at this time of year."

"But why?"

"Because of the herring." She sighed.

"But what about the herring?" Mark pressed her.

"Well, that stream out there happens to be a herring run. Every spring the herring swim up it from the ocean, against the current and rapids, and they jump up waterfalls and everything. They're trying to get back to the freshwater pond where they were born, to spawn there. For some reason they won't spawn anywhere else."

"And the gulls?"

"Well, the gulls just go crazy. At low tide the creek is just packed with herring. So they keep grabbing them and eating them and eating them. And even when they can't eat anymore they're so excited that they keep grabbing them and just dropping them down on the ground to die." A new wave of nausea ran through her, choking her voice to a stop.

"But the herring," Mark said. He sounded disturbed. Why should he get so upset about something like that? Lillian wondered. She had never seen him so talkative. "Do any of them get through?" Mark went on.

"Yes, yes, enough fish get through," Lillian said impatiently. "Each one lays about a million eggs anyway." She held her head in her hands. "I feel so sick! And why are we just sitting here, wasting time like this?" She sighed again. "We've got to do something about this mess, all of us. Come on." She pushed herself up out of her seat and carried some dishes into the kitchen.

"Oh!" she cried, almost dropping the dishes, "Oh, no, the ice cream!"

"What?" Jerry came into the room with the casserole in his hands. "Now what's happened?"

She was standing by the refrigerator, staring helplessly at a sagging ice cream carton and a great white pool on the avocado counter. Slowly, methodically, the melted ice cream was dripping down into a larger pool on the floor.

"How did that happen?"

"Oh, I must have left it out by mistake last night. And that spilled wine in the other room, how are we ever going to get it off the rug?" For a moment she felt like sagging down onto the floor herself. "I hate my parents!" she said vehemently. "Here, you clean this up. I'll finish clearing the table." And she strode into the other room.

Mark was still sitting down with his elbows on the table and his hands over his eyes. "Well, Mark," she said, rattling silverware noisily, "why are you just sitting there?"

Without moving, he mumbled, "I didn't come on this trip to clean house. I get enough of that at home."

"Well, you're going to!" Lillian insisted. "You made this mess as much as I did!"

Mark looked up at her, his cheeks blazing. He stood up quickly, pushing back his chair.

"And don't scrape the chair like that!" Lillian shouted. "You'll tear the rug!"

Mark made an unintelligible noise, more like a growl than anything else, and with heavy footsteps raced through the kitchen and out of the house, slamming the door behind him. Jerry and Lillian hurried to the kitchen window to see Mark running blindly down the path.

And then the phone rang.

"They *would* call now," Lillian moaned. She picked up the receiver. "Hello? Oh, hi." She nodded, with a grimace, at Jerry. "Fine, fine. . . . It's been raining a lot. . . . No, no, the house is warm." Oh, why did they treat her like such an infant? "I have tons of blankets. . . ." But wait, what was her mother saying? At first the words conveyed no meaning at all, but gradually their significance became clear. They weren't coming back tonight or even tomorrow night. Her mother wanted her to call a cab, go to the bus station, and come right to New York.

"Oh, but I don't want to!" was Lillian's first reaction. "I don't want to spend the whole vacation in the city."

With you, she almost added, but stopped herself in time. But what did she expect to do there, all by herself, for two whole days and nights, her mother wanted to know. And food, Lillian couldn't cook a thing, how was she going to eat? And would she really feel comfortable there, all alone, for two more nights? No, her mother was afraid she had to insist.

"But what about the Brockles?" Lillian said suddenly. "I could take a cab to their house, they're just in the next town, and stay there overnight."

There was silence on the other end of the phone. Then her mother began again. She didn't understand why it was so important to Lillian to stay, there would be a whole weekend left when they came back before school started, she had never seemed to like it there so much before, etc. etc. Lillian didn't really understand herself, but she wasn't going to give in.

"But why *can't* I stay at the Brockles' at night until you come back? You know they wouldn't mind."

"But we hardly know the Brockles," her mother explained. "And anyway, they're year-round people. They're not the same as people like us who just come to the country for the summer. How can you be so sure they'll have you?"

"*I* know them," Lillian pleaded. "You know

they like having a lot of kids around, there've always been guests there the times I've visited them."

Her mother sighed, paused, and finally consented, although she didn't know why she should, she added.

"Oh, thank you!" Lillian cried. "Everything will be perfect, you'll see."

Her mother repeated the usual admonitions, mentioned that she and her father were on their way out of the apartment and wouldn't be back until quite late tonight (she could hear her father in the background telling her to hurry), concluded with a final worry or two, and at last hung up.

"Parents!" Lillian said disgustedly.

"What happened?"

"Oh, they're not coming back for two more nights and they wanted me to go right home. But I couldn't stand to. And she's right, I don't love the country all that much, but I just wasn't expecting to be back in the apartment with them again so soon. I never get a chance to be away from them . . . And there're these people in the next town who we met last summer, and I sort of got to know them. They live here all year. I always wanted to go over there more, they have a lot of kids and a big house and friends are always dropping in and staying there; it's like a constant open house. I always wished my mother would let me spend the night there; they did invite me once; everybody is so relaxed about everything, not like my parents. And now I can!"

"Mmmm," said Jerry, peering anxiously out the window.

"Oh yes," Lillian said. "Mark. What's wrong with him, anyway?"

Jerry didn't seem to know what to say. "He's just . . . he just does this sometimes. It doesn't mean anything."

"How weird," Lillian murmured, preoccupied with her mother's neatly written little book of phone numbers. "Here it is, 'Brockle.' Isn't it a funny name?" It was strange how she had forgotten about them completely since the summer before, but now she was beginning to remember all the charming things about these people, and the casual way they lived which she had envied, and wished to be part of. The anticipation of being with them, and the knowledge that she wouldn't see her parents until the day after tomorrow were beginning to make her quite cheerful. She dialed, then waited, humming. There was a click, a blurred tone, and a voice said, "I'm sorry, the number you have dialed is no longer in service."

"But that's impossible," said Lillian. "Why would they — ?"

"I'm sorry," the voice repeated tonelessly, "the number you have dialed is no longer in service."

"Oh, shut up!" Lillian said to the recording, pressed the button, and dialed information. But the operator, sounding no less mechanical, informed her that there had been no listing under that name for six months.

"You mean they moved away or something?" This was, after all, the first attempt at contact she had made with the Brockles since moving back to the city last fall.

"I'm sorry, honey," the operator droned maddeningly, "we don't have that kind of information."

"But —" said Lillian.

" 'Bye now," said the operator, and hung up.

Lillian let the receiver drop slowly onto the hook. But that meant . . . that meant she was in the same situation all over again, except worse, for the boys really had to be somewhere tonight, and there were two nights now for her to be alone. The headache and nausea that she had forgotten flowed back into her. All of a sudden she remembered the radio (why hadn't she asked her mother about it?) and her mind became a well of hopelessness and confusion. She turned to Jerry, who was ineffectually wiping the ice cream off the counter.

"Do you think, do you think Mark will come back?" she asked him.

"Oh, of course," he said vaguely.

Lillian wondered if she were going to cry. "Well, he'd better!" she burst out. It was the only thing she could think of to say.

Eight

Jerry often was right about Mark, Lillian reflected as she stood, mop in hand, gazing at the kitchen floor, which was rather streaky from her hurried and superficial mopping. Mark had come back only a few moments later, apologizing, and had pitched right in with them. In fact, he had worked even harder than she or Jerry. He was just sort of emotional, she guessed, and got upset easily — although he did seem strangely suspicious of her, why, she could not understand.

And now, at last, the house was back in reasonable shape. But oh, how she hated cleaning up! Her mother seemed to love it; neither of her parents could bear the sight of a speck of dust. It was even worse in New York. Her mother had the apartment thoroughly cleaned each day, supervising the maid's every move. When company came over she was always emptying ashtrays. None of Lillian's friends' parents were like that; many of them lived quite comfortably in what her parents would consider the most depressing squalor, with children's toys lying around and books and newspapers left spread out on tables and the floor. And even though she had been brought up with it, Lillian could not adjust to her parents' compulsive need for order and cleanliness. It was simply against her nature.

Which was why, even now, after an hour of drudgery (made worse by the fuzzy nausea that was still with her), she could not really feel sure that the house was in perfect shape. Neither she nor the boys could think of one more thing to clean, yet she knew that her parents would be sure to find something wrong when they came back. The wine stain on the rug under the table, for instance. Unless you got down on the floor and searched for it, it was invisible to the naked eye. But she knew her parents would find it sooner or later.

"Well, I don't care!" she said aloud, banging the mop on the floor and making a small soapy puddle. She dragged the mop and the bucket, slopping over at the edges, into the cozy room, to leave by the doorway until the floor was dry. "You were right, Mark, when you said you didn't go on a trip to clean house. I don't want to spend all my time here cleaning house either. I mean, it's just wrong to have a house by the sea and want it to be perfectly clean all the time. I don't care what they think. And from now on, if it gets a little messy, I'm just going to force myself not to worry about it." She collapsed into a chair at the dining table, where the two boys were already slumped down.

"Well," said Jerry, "at least you'll only have one person to clean up after from now on." He turned to Mark. "We should really get going, we're going to have to ride like fury to get to Hugo's in time."

This was the moment Lillian had been dreading. Although the sky was heavy with clouds, the rain had stopped, and all the time they had been cleaning up she had been turning different solutions over and over in her mind. None of them were any good, and she had at last come to the conclusion that the only thing she could do was to throw herself at their mercy, tell them she was frightened, and beg them to stay. The trouble with that was that they would just tell her to go home, which, of course, she could always do. But she really didn't want to go home, and the rational part of her mind still told her that it was probably ridiculous to be afraid — she was hoping she could make herself stay even if they left, frightening though it might be. She knew their vacation was as long as hers, however, so they had the time if they would only change their plans, and it would be so much fun (with Jerry, at any rate), if they stayed. She had to make one last try.

But just as she was about to speak, having worked herself up to give an emotional, perhaps even tearful plea, Mark turned to her. "That stream out there, that herring run?"

"Uh . . . yes?" she said, not knowing what to expect.

"Well, I was wondering. . . ."

"Go on, go on, she urged, hardly daring to believe that some avenue of hope might come from *him*.

"Well, I keep thinking about it, about those

fish, trying to get away from the gulls, and then swimming upstream and all. . . ."

He was hesitant, as though it embarrassed him to talk about his feelings. Lillian was leaning forward in her chair, smiling at him, nodding her head quickly up and down to encourage him.

His eyes were on the table. "And I was wondering if . . . if it would be possible to maybe walk up the stream, and sort of watch the fish, and see what their pond is like, and how many of them get to it."

She couldn't believe it. Mark, who had always been so eager to leave, now wanted to stay. And if they went on the walk, there was a good chance she could drag it out long enough so that they wouldn't have time to get to Jerry's friend's.

"Oh," she said, "I'm sure we can do it."

"But, Mark," Jerry said, "how can we possibly do that? We hardly have enough time as it is."

"Oh, it's not a very long walk, I know. The pond is just up the hill." Lillian put in quickly.

"It really isn't that far to Hugo's, Jerry," Mark said. "You know that's why they said we could go. It's only about half a day's ride from here. And this herring run only happens once a year, isn't that what you said, Lillian?"

"Yes! Only once a year. Just for a few days."

"We'll never have this chance again," Mark went on, "and I really want to see it."

"So do I," said Lillian. "Really."

Obviously Jerry didn't like to argue. "Well, all right. I just hope we can make it."

This might not be so bad after all, Lillian said to herself as they started down the path, for there was a pleasant feeling of adventure to the trip. The two boys, walking ahead of her in ill-fitting castoff ponchos of her parents, made her feel that she was in some sort of strange, medieval procession; and in the unusual midday gloom her backyard was a damp and mysterious jungle.

Just as they were stepping out from under the trees onto the marsh, Lillian heard a noise behind her. She glanced back. There was quick movement among the trees, and suddenly something — or someone — darted behind a thick clump of underbrush.

"Wait!" she said. For an instant her knees almost gave way, and a feeling like a cold, wet fist slammed into her stomach. The boys turned back. "Did you see that?"

"See what?" Mark said impatiently, as though he couldn't bear to pause for one moment.

"There was . . . something in the trees. It might have been a person, hiding."

"Are you sure?" Jerry said. "Why would somebody be hanging around in the woods?"

"But I saw. . . ." Lillian's heart was beginning to beat slowly again. Suddenly she felt foolish, and a little angry, though still alarmed. She hurried to catch up with them. "But it might have been something. I never saw anything like it here before. And don't forget about the radio."

"Are you still thinking about that?" Mark said over his shoulder, already walking again.

Jerry and Lillian followed a few paces behind. She looked back into the trees, but could see nothing now. "But don't you understand?" she pleaded. "I really saw something. I think it must have been a person. What would anyone be doing there?"

"If you really saw someone, you'd know it," Jerry said. "Really, Lillian, I'm sure it was just . . . just. . . ."

"Just what? I don't know what else it could be. Why don't you believe me?"

"Because it doesn't sound that serious," he said in the superior tones of one who knows. "And I didn't see anything."

"Well I did, I know I did," Lillian murmured, almost to herself, thinking how hateful even he could be.

Once away from the beach, the stream wandered in wide curves through the flat, open expanse of marshland. To the right and left, rounded hills covered with gray trees rose like islands from the sea of tall grasses. The sky was black with clouds, yet the sun managed to penetrate them with an unearthly perpetual twilight. The only sound was the wind in the grass, and a distant rumble of surf.

Mark strode along the edge of the stream, continually peering down into its deep bed. He stopped for a moment and they caught up with him. "There's fish in there all right," he said. "Look."

In the dark flowing water were dark flowing shapes, the small narrow fish undulating as they fought the current. They were moving slowly, but they never stopped to rest.

"It's really amazing, the way they fight against the current like that," Mark said softly.

"I guess so," said Lillian. Actually, it *was* rather strange. She had always known about the herring, but never really thought about them before. Now, their struggling pulled at some responsive cord inside her, so that she almost felt compassion for them.

"God, they work hard," Jerry said. "It makes me tired just to look at them."

"A lot of them *do* seem to get past the gulls," Mark went on, as if he hadn't heard, and started walking again.

The creek skirted the foot of one of the hills, and when they came around it they could see that the marshland ended at a road some distance away. It was the main road, from which, far to their left now, Lillian's road broke away toward the sea. Beyond it the land rose gently, covered with trees. At the edge of the road an ungainly house with vibrant blue-metal siding extended out into the marsh, resting on large, raw cement pilings that had been built up over the spongy turf. It stood out quite boldly in an area where most buildings were faced with weathered wooden shingles and blended into the landscape.

As they approached the road, the creek, which had been quite wide, began to split apart into smaller streams, many of them hidden in the tall grass. They were deep, like small, twisting canyons, and after Jerry stepped right into one, slipping suddenly down into cold mud, the three of them watched the ground as they tried to weave their way through the intricate network. The ground was even damper here, Lillian's boots were full of water, and in order to progress they had to walk in wide loops to find channels that were narrow enough to jump across. Lillian was getting cold, and it seemed to be taking them forever to get to the road. She hated it. And although she struggled to keep herself from getting angry, it began to get more and more difficult to control a growing resentment toward Mark.

It was almost as if he had said to her, "I'll only stay with you if you'll wade through all this horrible mud," and somehow it seemed unfair.

"Gee, I just love wading through cold mud," she said, when at last they reached the blue house, wiping her boots on the cement.

"What a horrible building this is," Jerry said quickly.

"Isn't it?" said Mark. "I hate the way it sticks into the marsh. You can't look at the marsh at all without seeing it. Why didn't they just build it on the other side of the road?"

"They're building a lot of houses like that around here now," Lillian stated.

Mark glared at her.

"Come on," Jerry said, stepping between them. "Let's not stand here all day."

The stream ran through a wide corrugated metal pipe under the road. On the other side the ground was solid, and the water splashed in a rocky bed through pine woods, the trees stunted and bent at first, but growing taller and straighter as they went on. This was much pleasanter going, and the scenery was prettier than the marsh, to Lillian's eyes.

Mark still seemed to be fascinated by the fish. There were plenty of them to see, and he kept stopping to look. Even though she was still annoyed, Lillian couldn't help but be amazed at how steadily the fish, small as they were, kept going against the strong current. But she certainly wasn't going to admit it to Mark!

"Hey!" said Mark. "Listen. What's that noise?"

Coming from around a bend in the creek ahead, above the rustling of the water, were the sounds of many high-pitched voices, shouting and squealing. For an instant Lillian was reminded of the cries of the gulls, but she quickly realized that these were the voices of children.

"It sounds like a lot of kids," she said.

"Well, let's go and find out what's happening there," Jerry said. "What are we waiting for?"

Gradually a path appeared by the side of the stream. For a short while it turned from the water, and they followed it up a steep incline between high bushes which led finally to a wide clearing. They stopped.

From the vantage point of a small hill they could see that here the stream ran over several small, steep waterfalls. A series of rectangular cement pools had been built, each slightly higher than the one before, to form an alternate path for the herring so that they would be able to avoid the falls. It would have been a beautiful spot, with boulders, the falls, and a few willow trees bending over the stream, if it hadn't been for the people who filled the clearing. They were mostly young children armed with nets, who ran shrieking from one pool to the next dragging large buckets behind them.

"What's going on?" Lillian murmured.

"I know what's going on, Mark said slowly. "They're . . . they're fishing. They're catching the herring."

"But why?" said Lillian. "They're too small to eat."

"For the fun of it, of course," Mark said, and moved quickly down into the crowd.

Lillian found that she had to thread her way carefully through the people. There were so many, and as they hurried noisily about, wide-eyed and breathless, pushing through to the best places on the water, they did not bother trying to avoid bumping into each other. She worked her way to the edge of the water, where dead fish lay trampled into the mud. There a girl of about eight was squatting with a bucket beside her. The bucket was almost full to the brim with herring, some of them still squirming.

"What are you going to do with those fish?" Lillian shouted at her. It was the only way to make herself heard above the voices of the crowd.

The girl seemed surprised. "Um . . . I don't know," she shouted back. "Sometimes our cat eats them, I guess. Once my father tried putting some in the garden to make the flowers grow better."

But her attention span was short, and she turned quickly back to the stream. As Lillian watched, the girl casually dipped her net into the water, and, avoiding the dead fish floating on the surface, pulled out two struggling ones and deposited them into the bucket. She smiled up at Lillian. "That makes thirty-two," she said.

"How *wonderful*!" Lillian replied with heavy sarcasm, and swept away from her, colliding at once with a fat, panting man in an orange poncho. The water was lined with goggle-eyed people, avidly reaching for the fish, shrieking at each other, walking obliviously over the silvery corpses strewn along the bank; and the fish, in their efforts to get from one pool to the next, were literally jumping into the nets. And where were Jerry and Mark?

At last she caught sight of the two boys walking toward a pond at the top of the slope. She hurried to catch up with them. It was quieter by the pond; there were fewer people there. Mark and Jerry were staring into the water, and Mark's mouth had that tight, pinched look.

"What a hideous thing to find in the middle of the woods," said Lillian. "All those awful screaming people."

"Isn't it *terrible*?" Jerry said, with a bit too much drama in his voice. "Those poor fish, they get almost to the end, and then *people* come and kill them, for no reason."

They both looked at Mark. Well why doesn't he say something? thought Lillian.

Mark continued to stare into the water. "I saw a sign," he said softly after a short silence. "Only people who live in the town are allowed to fish here, and only four days a week. And some fish get through, they really do, I can see them in the pond." He paused. "But come on," he said abruptly, "let's get out of here. We're going to be late to Hugo's as it is," and he turned and started walking quickly away.

He can't bear it, thought Lillian, following him. He's really angry and upset, but it's not even about himself!

When they reached the house, the television was gone.

Nine

"Wait a minute," Lillian said, the cold feeling coming back to her stomach. Still in her poncho, she hurried into the living room to check on the television's usual place. It wasn't there. "But it was here, wasn't it?" she asked, coming back to the cozy room. "Right here on the table."

"Yes, it was," Jerry said.

"But . . . but I don't get it," she said. The cold feeling was spreading down to her knees. "It must mean. . . ." She didn't want to say it, but neither did they. "It must mean that someone. . . ." And at last she couldn't help herself. She took a deep breath. ". . . that it's been stolen."

For a moment no one spoke. They were all staring down at the table now, as if somehow that could make the television magically appear. The room filled with an expectant, breathless silence.

Upstairs, the door slammed again. Lillian jumped, her knees almost giving way, and her eyes darted to the ceiling. Were there footsteps?

"The radio," Mark said softly.

Lillian's heart began to pound. "The radio?" she repeated, not yet understanding, but knowing it meant something terrible. "The radio?"

And then she remembered. "That's right, the radio." Was her voice shaking? "I was sure I saw it yesterday. And it's been working perfectly. My parents didn't take it with them. It's been stolen too." Unsteadily she sank into a chair, her hand clutching at its back.

The two boys, still standing, were staring at her now. Jerry cleared his throat. "The strange thing," he said hesitantly, "if it's true — is that they were taken at different times. It means that someone's been in the house twice, without our knowing about it."

"And the other thing," Mark began. Lillian was shaking her head. She didn't want to hear anymore; every time someone spoke it just got worse. But Mark went on. "The other thing is that they were both taken while we were away. Which must mean that — "

"Someone's been watching us," Lillian interrupted, her eyes moving from face to face. "Someone's out there, watching us." The coldness had moved to her fingers now, and she was twisting her hands together. "In the woods this morning, don't you remember, I thought I saw something in the woods. Something hiding. Waiting for us to — "

"Hey!" Mark said suddenly, and Lillian jumped again. He turned to Jerry, running his hand across his forehead. "Now I remember. Last night, when I went outside for the bikes, I thought I saw something. . . ." His voice trailed off.

"What?" Lillian said, holding her arms against her chest to keep from trembling, for the cold feeling was in her whole body now. "What did you see?"

"It was hard to tell." He was still looking at Jerry. "It was just a shape, a dim shape, moving through the trees. . . ."

In the moment that followed, while the three of them watched each other, the rain began again, its sound growing in waves that came beating against the house. It was a lonely sound, reminding Lillian of how isolated they were, with only the wind and the sea outside, and how vulnerable. She imagined the shadows, and the trees, and a dark figure, faceless, watching the house, waiting; and then moving purposefully toward it. And it's real, a voice kept repeating inside her head. It's not just your imagination. It's real.

"But this doesn't make sense," Jerry said.

"Doesn't it?" Lillian asked hopefully, still shivering.

"I mean, why would anybody be lurking around outside in the rain just to get a stupid radio?" He sounded as though he was trying to persuade himself that it wasn't really happening. "It's crazy."

"Crazy?" Lillian said, rocking slightly in her chair, still clasping her arms, and trying not to think. "Yes, it is crazy, isn't it? Only a crazy person would do it. What if — " she stopped to take a breath, to control her voice. " — what if it's somebody who escaped from an insane asylum? Maybe it is." Her eyes kept moving from their faces to the table to the window to their faces again, never pausing on anything, trying not to see their frightened expressions or the tossing trees outside. "It must be a crazy person, nobody else would — "

"No," said Mark. "It couldn't be. What would a crazy person want with a radio and a TV? You're just going to scare all of us if you talk that way."

"But I am scared," Lillian said softly, her voice hollow in the quiet of the room. "I'm scared to death." Nervously, she pushed her hair out of her eyes. "I want to tell my parents. Oh, but they'll die when they find out. And they'll blame me, they'll say I'm irresponsible. But they would know what to do."

"But what could they do?" said Jerry.

"I know what they'd do," Lillian said hopelessly. "My mother would scream at me. First they'd be mad about the TV, then when I explained about it they'd get scared. My mother would start crying. My father would start giving me orders to close the house and take the cab to the bus." She stopped suddenly. "But I can't call them! My mother said they wouldn't be home until late."

"But isn't there anyone else around here you could go and stay with?" Mark asked.

"The only year-round people we know here are the Brockles, and they're gone," said Lillian. "Nobody else we know ever opens up their houses this early. There's nobody."

"But why can't you just take the bus to New York, like your parents would want?" Jerry asked her.

"Because the bus left. There's only one bus and it's in the morning. I have to stay." She shook her head again, trying to understand what was happening. "There's nothing I can do."

She looked at Jerry beseechingly, hoping he would offer to stay, but he turned away, biting his lip. His face was drawn and colorless in the cold gray light. For a moment no one spoke. The wind moved fiercely in the trees, as if warning them of danger, suddenly bringing closer the shrieking of the gulls and the heavy surf. All night, alone in the dark, she would be hearing those gulls, waiting, listening for the door to open, for footsteps. She would have to run away, out into the rain and the blackness, a helpless figure on the long, empty road. The sound of her heartbeat filled her ears, and she felt sweat breaking out on her forehead. Her eyes were moving again; she didn't know where to look.

Mark sighed, and her eyes flew to his face. Slowly, with resignation, he slipped off his poncho, hung it over the back of a chair, and sat down. He looked up at Jerry, who was still standing. "You better call Hugo," he said. "We're going to have to stay."

"Stay?" said Jerry. "But how can we? We're supposed to be there for dinner. And it's not safe here, with that person outside."

"But that's why we have to stay," Mark insisted. "We can't leave her here alone. I don't want to stay any more than you do."

Nervously, Jerry flashed Lillian a faint smile. "But couldn't you . . . couldn't you . . . ?"

"I can't do anything. I already told you." Her pride, her desire to appear independent, were forgotten now. All she could feel was fear. "Please, please stay," she begged him. "You've got to. Please, Jerry."

"Well," Jerry said, with a strange little laugh, "I guess we do, then. I'll go call Hugo. But what should I say?"

"Don't ask me," said Mark, turning away. "You know him better than I do."

"Just say . . . ," Lillian said, "Just say. . . ."

"I mean," Jerry went on, "If I told the truth, his folks probably wouldn't want us to stay, they'd be worried, they'd call *my* folks, it would all be a big mess."

Lillian's mind was racing. She had to get him to call, as soon as possible, for only then could she be sure they would stay. But what could he say to Hugo? "Just say," she continued, "Say . . . I know! That you met somebody at the hostel, that's where you were supposed to be last night, right?"

"Yes," Jerry said, watching her doubtfully.

"Somebody who . . . did you ever go to camp or anything?"

"For about two weeks. Then I quit. I hated it."

"Well, say you met somebody from camp, make up a name." She was searching frantically for ideas. "And he has a house near here, and invited you to stay, and you're going to. What's wrong with that?"

"Nothing. I guess. . . ."

"Then call him."

Jerry called him. Lillian stood up as she listened to him talking into the kitchen wall phone, her apprehensions sinking away again. They would be here at least another night; for the moment she was safe. She let her wet poncho drop to the floor, feeling relieved for the second time in two days. Jerry came back, dropped his poncho onto the rug, and sat down.

Mark was tapping his heel restlessly on the floor. "Why did you ever call this the 'cozy' room?" His eyes roamed around the sterile, barren room with its prim white curtains and a few colorless engravings on the walls. "It's about the most *un*cozy place I've ever been in."

"Because it's always the warmest room in the house," Lillian said, a bit insulted by his remark, even though she herself was always criticizing her parents' taste.

"I guess we're just going to be sitting here all day again, aren't we?"

"Well, we could eat lunch," Lillian said brightly, getting up, trying to make them feel as relieved as she was. "I'll see what there is."

What there was, as it happened, wasn't much — not even the usual lunchtime standbys like tuna fish or canned soup or peanut butter. "I'm sorry," Lillian said to them, leaning in the kitchen doorway and feeling foolish. "There's hardly anything to eat. I guess my mother was planning to bring more food today. . . ."

"Is there a store anywhere near here?" Mark asked.

"Well, yes, but it's a few miles up the road."

"I'll go get some food," he said, quickly standing up. "I don't mind getting wet."

After about two miles, the road that ran past Lillian's house met the coast road, where Mark, on his bike, made a right and soon reached the store. It turned out to be the same blue building they had noticed disfiguring the marsh that morning. The front of the store was rather nice, he thought; it was old and wooden, with large arched windows and lots of gingerbread carving. Inside, a group of big-bellied men lounged near the cash register, perusing a gun catalogue and joking with the woman behind the counter, who had dark bobbed hair and became very efficient when Mark approached her.

"That's the old part," she said coldly to him, when he told her rather timidly that he liked the front of the store. "We're getting rid of that any day now. We've expanded. We have a whole new addition now. We'll be moving out of this old place right away," and she gestured, the flesh on her upper arm quivering, to indicate the original interior: dark wooden shelves, a wide counter with a large spool of string on it that looped through a hook on the ceiling, a fat black stove in the corner. The new part, he could see, gleamed with plastic and glass, and looked exactly like any store in the city.

They had mostly canned foods, and he filled his pack with tuna fish and peanut butter and beans and spaghetti with meatballs, as well as milk and bread and some eggs. He coasted almost all the way back.

After a lunch of peanut butter sandwiches (Jerry put lettuce and mayonnaise on his), the afternoon crept by with a desultory silence among the three of them, the eerie, aggressive screaming of the gulls filling the quiet of the house. They wandered aimlessly about the room, unable to read, or wash the dishes or think of anything else to do, or even to think of what to say to each other. Surreptitiously one would glance out into the backyard, then turn quickly away, not wanting the others to see.

At last Mark was able to persuade Lillian to let him bring the bikes into the storeroom by the back door, and whistling, sitting cross-legged, he spent the rest of the afternoon cleaning and polishing them. For Jerry and Lillian, who remained in the cozy room, the time consisted of more boredom and inertia, mixed with half-hearted bickering.

"God, it's cold in here," Jerry whined toward the end of the afternoon.

"The heat's as high as it will go."

"Can't we have a fire?"

"There's no wood," Lillian snapped back.

"But there must be wood somewhere, look at all those trees out there."

"Well, there is a big woodpile down in the back, but it's all wet, of course. It might burn, if someone's willing to make the effort."

"I'll build the fire," Mark called out to them.

"If you cook the dinner, I'll go out and get some wood," Lillian said.

"Sure," said Jerry.

They got up and went into the kitchen, and Lillian disappeared out the back door. "Let's see," Jerry said to himself, "tuna fish." He took a cookbook from a shelf and thumbed through it. "Hmm," he murmured, "creamed tuna with eggs, tuna-noodle bake, tuna cheese surprise —"

And then they heard Lillian scream.

Ten

Lillian had stepped out onto the porch and down the steps to the lawn, letting the door bang behind her. The lawn was soft and spongy under her bare feet, and the path was slippery with mud. Though glad that the boys were staying, she was still worried, of course, about the television and the radio. As the sticks and stones in the path bit into her feet, she considered the situation, with irritation, for the hundredth time. What were her parents going to think, in the first place? Her father probably would be furious, she knew how he prized his possessions; and he would blame her for not being careful, not locking the doors. And Jerry and Mark, what about them? Should she tell her parents they had been staying in the house? Her mother would have a fit, she was sure. But if she didn't tell them, her mother would probably be just as upset that she had stayed by herself in what might be a dangerous situation.

She kicked a stone into the underbrush, then

cursed under her breath with the pain it caused. That was the other worry about Jerry and Mark. Had she lured them into danger? If something happened to them, would it be her fault? Why hadn't she just stayed by herself and then gone home this morning, as her mother had wanted? If only she had known this was going to happen!

And were they really in danger? Was someone actually watching them? It must be true, for there could be no doubt that the radio and TV had been taken. But perhaps that was all the thief had wanted; perhaps he would not come back again. Oh, please don't let him come back, Lillian begged silently, clasping her hands as she hurried among the trees in the fading light.

The surf made a mournful sound, and the small hollow at the bottom of the yard was quite dark now. She wished she had brought a flashlight. The large pile of wood was wedged between two trees at the very lowest point, and when she reached it she turned around for a moment to look up at the house. There was a light in the kitchen window, but all the others were dark, giving the gray building a deserted, forbidding look, as if there were no comfort even there. She turned quickly and pulled a large log from the pile. There was a face behind it.

A pale, narrow face with wide eyes staring crazily into her own, and a thin mouth that moved. Like a bird hypnotized by a snake she stood frozen, clutching at the log, staring into the eyes, while around her the trees swayed and sighed. The mouth opened; a hoarse whisper came out of it. Lillian screamed and dropped the log and began to run up the hill, through the trees, screaming, screaming, stumbling and falling, forgetting her feet and the stones and the underbrush, forgetting the path, running for the light in the kitchen window.

Mark was all the way across the lawn and starting into the trees by the time she reached him; Jerry was several yards behind. "Hurry!" she screamed as Mark grabbed her arm, "Inside, we've got to get inside! He's following me, he's following me, he's right behind!" Clumsily grasping each other, they stumbled toward the house, up the steps, into the door, Mark slammed it behind them and Lillian clicked the lock, then fastened the chain. She turned around. The two boys were staring at her with their mouths open. Slowly, her back against the door, she sank down onto the floor.

"What happened?"

"I saw him. He was staring at me."

"Are you sure?" Mark said softly.

"Yes! It wasn't like before. I really saw him, a few feet away from me. I — I took a piece of wood out of the pile, and there was this face behind it, twitching, and — and just staring at me. Oh, it was horrible!" She buried her head in her hands, shaking it back and forth.

When the boys didn't say anything she lifted her head. They were standing motionless, looking at each other with white faces. "It was a crazy person," she said. "I know it. He was hiding there. And he's probably right outside!" She jumped up and peered through the narrow window beside the door. It was completely dark now, and she could see nothing but the twisted trees against the sky. "Oh, what are we going to do?" she said, feeling herself begin to cry.

"Did he say anything?" said Mark. "Did he try to hurt you? Did he come after you?"

"Oh, I don't know." Tears were welling up in her eyes, and her nose was running, but she ignored it. "He started to — " she gulped, " — he started to say something, but I ran away. And I kept thinking he was following me, but maybe he wasn't, I don't know." The tears were running down her cheeks now. "He didn't try to hurt me, I guess. In fact — in fact he seemed scared too. But his eyes, his eyes, they were so . . . so crazy." She covered her eyes with her hands again. "Oh, God," she said, and began to sob.

"Maybe we should get out of here," Jerry said in a cracked voice, and cleared his throat.

"But what about me?" Lillian moaned. "I can't get out of here. I have no place to go anymore." She paused to gasp for breath. "And now you want to leave." She retreated again behind her hands. Somehow, when she couldn't see anything, she felt a little safer, as though she were hiding under the blankets.

"Well, let's not just stand here all night," said Mark. "It's warmer in the other room." Lillian followed slowly behind them, wiping her eyes. They looked out of the window and then sat down, as always, around the table, which was covered with crumbs and dishes and crusted blobs of mayonnaise from lunch. Suddenly Lillian felt that she'd spent her whole life sitting with Jerry and Mark around this table.

"But isn't there someplace else you could go?"

Jerry said. "I mean, we really should get out of here now."

"Oh, I don't know," she said. "I can't think. I just keep seeing that face."

There was a silence.

"Maybe we don't have to leave," Mark said.

"What?" Jerry said, turning so abruptly to face him that his chair moved. "What do you mean?"

"Don't scrape the chair on the rug," Lillian said dully.

"But what do you mean, Mark? I mean, I don't see how we could possibly stay here, with that crazy person outside."

"But . . . how do we *know* he's crazy?" Mark said slowly, gathering speed as he went on. "How do we know anything about him? How do we know he's the same person who took the radio and the TV? Maybe he was just taking a walk and when he saw Lillian he tried to hide because he was on private property. People sometimes shoot trespassers, you know."

"Sure," Lillian said. "And if he came screaming up the path waving a scythe at me you'd say he was just paying a friendly call." She sighed and fell back into her chair. "I don't get you at all."

And then, all at once, she knew what they should do. It was so simple and obvious that she wondered why she hadn't thought of it immediately; it was so foolproof that relief suddenly flowed through her like a hot bath.

"But *I* know," she said. "All we have to do is call the police."

"Of course," said Jerry. "Why didn't we think of it before?"

"I have the number," Lillian said. "They'll come, and start looking around with flashlights, and if he's not out there they'll search until they find him, and they'll guard the house and everything, and try to find the stolen things. Then we'll be completely safe. And my parents will say I did just the right thing." She rose from her chair.

"Sit down," Mark said in a strange, hard voice. "You're not calling the police."

Eleven

"What?" said Jerry. "But Mark. . . ."

Lillian stood uncertainly behind her chair. Mark's words, the firm, toneless way he had said them, frightened her. His face, as usual, showed little expression, but a kind of fierce determination glittered in his eyes.

"She's not calling the police," Mark said, sounding strangely calm.

Lillian shivered, almost expecting him to announce that the man outside was his cohort, that they were about to murder both her and Jerry. "Yes, I am," she said in a small, shaky voice.

"No," said Mark.

"But why not?" she asked, eyeing him warily, studying his face for signs of madness. She clutched at the back of a chair to keep her hand from trembling.

"Because . . . because it might not be fair."

"Fair?" she said in bewilderment. "But who's thinking about fair? I'm thinking about not getting killed."

"But that's the whole point," said Mark. "Whatever gave you the idea you were going to get killed? Okay, so the radio and television are gone. Any kid could have taken them. And the guy behind the woodpile was probably scared to death when you saw him. Why else would he be hiding? He probably took off in the other direction faster than you did."

Jerry was sitting very uncomfortably on the edge of his chair, looking back and forth between them. He seemed to be about to say something, but Lillian spoke first. "But Mark, how do you know that? All we know is that somebody's really out there, somebody who acts crazy." Why was Mark doing this? It was terrifying, the way he was staring at her so stiffly. "I have to call," she went on, trying to make her voice steady. "Right now."

"You are *not* calling," Mark said firmly, standing up.

"Yes I *am*, and you can't stop me!" she insisted, feeling close to tears again, sticking out her chin. She didn't move, however; there was something oddly compelling about his voice.

Jerry was twisting on his seat in a kind of agony, forcing his facial muscles into a poor imitation of a smile. "Please, don't fight," he said. "Can't we just calmly discuss it?"

"What is there to discuss?" said Lillian, her voice beginning to break. It was terrible to have decided what to do and then have Mark so unreasonably try to stop her. She gestured at Mark, shaking her head. "He must be crazy or something."

Mark was growing very red in the face. "No, no," Jerry faltered, looking quickly at Mark. "He's just . . . please don't . . . let's try to — "

"But maybe we'll find out more about it," said Mark. "Can you just wait?"

"Wait?" she said. "Wait for what?" She looked to Jerry for help, but he was staring down at his lap, cringing against his chair. She'd get no help from him. He was always trying to be so nice, as though people were bombs that might go off if he said the wrong thing. "Wait for him to sneak in and cut our throats and take everything in the house?" she went on. "Is that what you want us to do? But I can't, Mark, I just *can't!* I've got to call! And anyway, it's my house. I don't have to listen to you." She was breathing heavily, and beginning to get angry. "It's my house and my things and I have to protect them, and I don't have to pay any attention to somebody I invited in and gave food to and everything."

"But who wants to stay here and eat your dumb food?" said Mark, his voice growing louder, but brokenly, as though it were an effort for him to speak at all. "You can have your old house, it wasn't me who wanted to stay here, we just did it to protect you; you can have your old house and every dumb ugly thing in it. If you call the police, I'm leaving."

"But Mark," Jerry pleaded miserably. "We — "

"Yes!" Lillian shouted, leaning farther forward, her head shaking. "And from the first second you were here you acted like you hated it, and like you hated me, and didn't want to help or anything. And you're just *crazy* and I'm not paying one bit of attention to you anymore." She straightened herself. "I. Am. Calling." She turned toward the kitchen.

Mark's face was bright red as he stood clenching and unclenching his fists. His whole body was tense, as though he were keeping himself from flying into a thousand pieces. "If you call I'll run out there and warn him, I'll yell that the police are coming. I'll yell so loud the whole woods will hear."

"Oh, calm down, creep," Lillian said, beginning to dial.

And then, so suddenly and quickly that she hardly knew what was happening, Mark raced at her, and with both hands pushed her to the floor. He turned to the phone, grabbed the receiver, and ripped it out of the wall.

Twelve

The hum of the refrigerator, the rain outside, the two bright spots on Mark's cheeks and the pain in her elbow were all that Lillian could concentrate on as she lay on the cold linoleum.

Cradling the receiver gently, as though it were a wounded bird, Mark turned and set it down on the counter. "I — " he said, spreading his arms in a hopeless gesture.

Lillian couldn't think of what to do or say. The surface of her mind was a blank above the dark well of confusion and fear. Then she caught sight of the broken telephone, the body of it pulled partway out of the wall, its plastic entrails exposed. Rubbing her elbow, she got to her feet and without a word walked quickly into the other room, to the window.

Jerry had hurried into the kitchen, and for a short, silent time the two boys remained by the phone. She did not turn when they came back to the cozy room, unable to tear her eyes from the window. Although the trees moving against the sky were barely visible, the darkness outside was alive. Perhaps it was the sounds of the rain and the surf and the screaming gulls that made the blank space beyond the window seem to pulsate and writhe, as though the very air were made of twisting snakes performing some terrible dance. It was not her yard she was looking at, but a black pit moving to engulf the now utterly vulnerable house, a pit from which at any moment the darker figure would rise up, a figure with a thin smile and a glittering knife.

She was not conscious of her hands twisting ceaselessly together, of the quivering at the back of her neck. She was not conscious of the boys sitting down behind her, until Jerry said, "Lillian."

She turned, her hands still twisting. The boys were hardly more than dark shapes in the unlit room; but Mark seemed stunned, staring down at the table, and Jerry was watching her apprehensively.

"Lillian?" Jerry said again.

"What are we going to do?" she murmured, despair in her voice. "What are we going to do?"

"Why don't you sit down?" said Jerry.

She ignored him. "He's out there, I know he's out there, and we can't do anything. He could come in anytime. He came in before." Her voice was very quiet and detached, sounding to her as though it were coming from far away. She turned back to the window.

Behind her there were footsteps, and suddenly the darkness was gone, replaced by the glaring reflection of the lamp, Mark's uncomfortable face looking at her, and Jerry, rippling in the glass, moving back to his seat.

She turned back to them. "Why did you turn on the light? Now we can't see outside."

Jerry sighed, sitting down. "What difference would it make anyway?"

Mark seemed more and more worried as he watched her. "Lillian," he said with an effort, "I'm sorry. I . . . I don't know what happened It was just. . . ."

She watched him silently, her hands still twisting.

"I just . . . couldn't help myself." He ran his hand over his forehead. "Maybe you should . . . go to bed, try to sleep. I'll stay up and watch, I'll stay awake. I won't let anything happen."

"But then. . . ." She was confused. The fear made it difficult for her to think. "But then you do think we're in danger, that somebody has to watch. But if you think we're in danger, then why did you, why did you do that to the phone?"

"Oh. . . ." He shifted in his seat, looking away from her. "Just, when you told about that person out there, he sounded so lonely, and hunted, and . . . helpless, and . . . and I just couldn't stand to think of policemen and dogs and everything, ripping up the bushes, hunting him down."

She couldn't understand. It was she who had seen the person, she who knew that he was a madman, and dangerous. Why hadn't he believed her? Why hadn't he seen that *they* were in danger, not the lurking maniac outside. And why had he waited until now to recognize their danger; now, when it was too late?

Jerry was trying to explain, gesturing. "It's just Mark's way. He's always on the side of the underdog. He's always been like that. And now," he glanced for a moment at Mark, "and now, I guess, he's on your side. Lillian, are you all right? You seem so strange."

"Please," Mark said with sudden urgency, studying her face again. "Please, just try to forget about it. Go to bed. Don't worry, please." He even seemed a bit annoyed with her. "We'll take care of everything."

Bed? It might be nice to go to bed at that, and at least try to forget, try to push away the gnawing ache of fear and leave it to them. After all, she said to herself, her mind beginning to clear a bit, it was Mark's fault. "Well . . . well, all right," she said, glancing once more at the window but seeing only the dim, dreary reflection, and her own thin face. "Yes . . . ," she murmured, and still twisting her hands, she hurried out of the room.

And it was true, it was better in bed, huddled under the blankets, away from the downstairs window, thinking of the boys awake and watching, taking care of her. Strangely, the wind and the creaking house seemed to be lulling her to sleep, though she was not really aware that she had fallen into a fitful doze until she was awakened by footsteps coming slowly up the stairs.

Whoever it was seemed to be looking into all the bedrooms. They were probably going to take turns watching, she thought drowsily, and one of them was looking for blankets. "Do you want some blankets?" she asked, sitting up in bed.

Someone walked into the room. But the figure in the doorway was too tall, his breathing was strangely heavy, his profile against the faint light behind was unfamiliar. It was not Jerry or Mark.

Thirteen

Lillian's stomach turned to ice. She felt herself begin to scream, but suddenly she stopped herself. If she screamed, he would try to shut her up, he would put his hand across her mouth, he would start to strangle her! *Don't scream!* she screamed inside her head, pushing her lips tightly together, staring with horror at the figure in the doorway, who was slowly turning toward her. And what, it suddenly hit her, *had* happened to Jerry and Mark? Why hadn't they tried to stop him? Had he done something to them? Were they *dead?*

At this thought, a wail began to push its way out of her throat; but somewhere it got stuck, and came out only as a choked gasp. The man was nearing the bed; she was pressing herself against the wall behind her pillow. Was it the man from the woodpile? In the darkness she couldn't see his face. And then he stopped moving and sat down on the chair beside the bed. For a moment he looked toward the stairs and the light shone dimly on his face. Then Lillian screamed.

It was the same face. She had expected it, but seeing again those long features, the tight, nervous mouth, brought back upon her the same shock of horror she had felt out in the darkness. For a moment she almost heard the trees sighing and the surf close by. He turned toward her again and rose out of the chair.

"No!" she said. "Please. I won't scream anymore. I promise. Don't. I won't scream. I won't. I won't."

Slowly he sat down, staring at her. His face was expressionless. If only he would say something! That blank face, staring at her. Why didn't he say anything? But if she talked, maybe he wouldn't come at her, maybe he would listen to her, maybe she could get him to go away.

"Um," she said. "Uh, this is, it's late, isn't it? But I won't tell anyone. I'll pretend I was asleep. Really. What could I tell them anyway, I hardly know what you look like, do I?" Oh, stop it, she moaned to herself, I do know what he looks like, and he knows it. He knows I could identify him. "But it's too dark to see your face now, and I didn't really see anything before," she went on quickly, "By the woodpile, I mean. It was too dark. I couldn't see your face then, if it was you. Really, I couldn't see it. I just screamed because, because it was so scary to suddenly see somebody there, when I wasn't expecting it. But all I could see was that somebody was there, I couldn't see your face. It was a nice face, though, what I could see." Flattery will get you nowhere, she thought, idiotically.

"But I mean, it was you, by the woodpile, wasn't it? I don't care, really. I don't care about the radio and TV either, if you took them. Mark thinks maybe you didn't take them, if that was you by the woodpile. In fact, in fact he wouldn't even let us call the police, and we didn't call the police, in fact he ripped — " Just in time she stopped herself.

He mustn't know there was no phone, then he would know how safe he was, he would know he could do anything to her and no one would know. And why had she told him they hadn't called the police? She should have said the police were waiting outside. It might have scared him away.

"But the police do come around here quite frequently," she lied. "I'm just warning you, to help you. I don't think you deserve to get caught. My parents have a lot of money, they can afford another TV and radio." Oh, God, why did she have to tell him *that?* Now he would think they were really rich, and might try to kidnap her. Kidnapping victims hardly ever came back alive. "My parents aren't rich, though. I mean, they could hardly afford this house, actually somebody gave it to them, and all the furniture and stuff, it's just from Goodwill. Really."

She stopped for breath. Blankly, the man continued to stare at her. If only he would say something! If only his lips would move! And yet, though there was no expression, she could feel the intensity of his stare.

Quickly she began again. "Well anyway, um, it's nice around here, don't you think? The sea and everything. My parents wanted me to go back to the city when they left, but — " There she went again, telling him how helpless she was! Why did she keep doing that? "But they'll be back any day. I mean, they'll be back tomorrow, they said. My mother will be hysterical about the TV. I don't know what to tell them. They'll never let me be on my own again, they'll say I'm irresponsible. But it's not only my fault, it's Jerry's and Mark's too. They're these two boys I met. I invited them to come in, and then it started raining, and they couldn't leave. Maybe you noticed them."

Maybe you *killed* them, she thought suddenly. What else could have happened? She hadn't heard any noise, any fighting. A chill ran through her. "Do — do you know where they are? Please tell me. I won't tell anyone, I promise." They had been watching for him. Why hadn't they seen him? Why hadn't they heard her scream? What had he done to them? She was crying. "Please tell me!"

The man's face was twitching. A black-gloved hand rose from his lap. Lillian couldn't bear it. He was going to kill her now!

"No!" she said. "Don't tell me. Don't. I'm sorry. Jerry and Mark. They. . . ." She had to stop talking about them! "I have this friend at school named Abigail," she continued frantically. "She's my best friend, I guess, but I hate her a lot of the time. She thinks she's so perfect. She's just as giggly and silly as anybody else, and likes to gossip and everything and gang up on people. But then whenever there're boys around she starts acting real mysterious and aloof, as if she's above all that. And of course all the boys fall for it. They think she's this inscrutable *mystery* or something, and better than other girls, but really she's just shy and doesn't have anything to say to boys. She just gets this vague smile and distant gaze in her eyes and I want to kick her. But she always denies it, of course, when I get mad at her about it, and starts crying."

She turned toward him, hardly conscious of what she had been saying. He was leaning toward her slightly, his hands on his knees. If only she knew what time it was! Was it getting light out? He would have to leave in the morning, he would just have to. But now she had to keep talking. Whenever she stopped he seemed to get restless, he seemed to want to do something. But she kept saying the wrong things. What could she talk about? And then she had an idea.

"We went for a walk today. We followed the brook that flows into the sea out behind the house. Did you know that it was a herring run? Do you know what that is?" And she began to explain about the fish fighting their way upstream to spawn. As she spoke she looked straight ahead, as if she were reciting a poem in school, sitting up in bed, her hands twisting under the blankets, with occasional quick glimpses toward the man in the chair. He was motionless now, staring into his lap. It was so difficult to talk when she had no idea what the other person was thinking.

"And you must have noticed how craz—I mean how strange the gulls are now. That's because of the herring. They've never seen so many fish all at once before and they can't control themselves, they just keep eating and eating them, and when they can't eat anymore they still grab them out of the stream and then throw them down on the ground to die. But the herring that make it past the gulls have to make it past the people, because at the end of their trip all these people are waiting to grab them with nets, for no reason — " She glanced over. He was looking up at her again. " — just for the fun of it, and to give to their cats, but not to eat. They're too small to eat. And all these horrid little girls are there, trying to get more than anybody else, and — "

Her voice seemed to freeze in her throat. He had started making some terrible noise. Slowly, cautiously, hardly daring to look, she turned to him. His lips were moving, his whole body was shaking. And that choking noise, it was laughter! The man was laughing! Lillian sat paralyzed in her bed as he rose to his feet. He stood above her, looking down on her, and suddenly his laughter stopped. Lillian stared at him, unable to think of a thing to say, wishing now, exhausted, that he would just kill her and get it over with.

His voice was hoarse, as though he hadn't spoken for days, and rough. "I'm sorry," he said. "I didn't mean to frighten you outside. That's all I wanted to tell you. Sometimes. . . ," he put his hand over his eyes, ". . . sometimes I hardly know what I'm doing. I only wanted to tell you, don't be afraid. And now I've scared you even more. It's. . . ." And he started laughing again. Oh, it was horrible! The laughter sounded like knives ripping his insides to shreds. She wanted to cover her ears. "I . . . don't be afraid," he said, and before she knew it he was out of the room and down the stairs.

Lillian collapsed onto her back. The sheets were soaking wet, and cold. She heard the back door close downstairs. It was over! He hadn't even touched her. It was over. She could hardly believe it. She couldn't understand what was happening. She noticed, between her sobs, that the room was getting light.

It was almost broad daylight before she had the courage to walk, on shaking legs, down the stairs, clutching her wrinkled nightgown about her, trying not to think what she would find. Jerry and Mark were sprawled across the table. There was no blood. Jerry lifted his head slowly as she approached. "Oh," he said, "Good morning. Did you sleep okay?"

"What!" she screamed, and Jerry leapt to this feet. "*What?* You mean this whole time you've just been *asleep?*"

Fourteen

She told them over and over again, of course, what had happened, describing every detail, repeating the entire conversation, word for word, as well as she could remember it. Jerry seemed to be endlessly fascinated, praising her effusively for her courage; but after a while Mark got bored, put on his poncho, and went to sit sullenly on the back porch in the drizzle.

Her parents had said they weren't coming back until the day after this. Yesterday she hadn't thought at all about what she would do today and tonight; it had been enough then to know that the boys were going to stay with her *that* night. Now, although Jerry had mentioned several times that they should probably get going, since they were expected at Hugo's, Mark seemed strangely indifferent, almost as though he didn't want to leave. Lillian knew that what she should obviously do was go to the store down the road and call the police, but somehow she kept not getting around to it, telling Jerry that she would do it in a little while.

She decided at last that when the boys left, she would go with them as far as the store, then wait there for the police to come. But the morning drew on, and Mark remained out on the porch. Jerry was clearly anxious to leave, continually looking at the clock, but after a while he just gave up trying to get Mark to move. As always, Lillian reflected, Jerry was treating Mark carefully; his insistence that they should leave seemed to irritate Mark, so Jerry stopped. What she couldn't understand was why Mark didn't want to get away as soon as possible; but since she didn't feel like pulling herself together just yet, she didn't question his behavior.

Jerry didn't seem to understand him either. "I just don't get it," he said. It was close to noon, the two of them were huddled around the fire that Mark, who was still out on the porch, had finally managed to build with wet wood he had gathered earlier. "I mean, you know how much he wanted to leave before, and they're expecting us at Hugo's; it'll be a real mess if we don't show up, and now it isn't safe here."

"Mmmm," said Lillian vaguely. "Yes, it is strange. But he's always strange, it seems to me." And I'm strange too, she thought, wondering again why she felt so reluctant to leave the house. "I wonder what he would have done if that man came into his room in the middle of the night," she went on. "He's the one it should have happened to, because he's the one who wanted to protect him. I wonder how brave he would have been."

"Shhh, he'll hear you." Jerry peered anxiously past her in the direction of the porch. "I don't know what he would have done," he continued, whispering, "but one thing you have to admit is that Mark is pretty brave. Once he gets an idea in his head and decides to do something about it, nothing can stop him. I'm the one who would have been too petrified to think." He was kneeling, his clasped hands bouncing up and down on his jeans. "God, I don't know how you could stand it. It must have been so horrible. And what's to stop him from coming back? I wish Mark would move, we've really got to get out of here, that guy could come back anytime. It's almost twelve already."

The sound was so unexpected that Jerry jumped, nearly toppling over. "A car!" Lillian said. "But my parents weren't supposed to come back until tomorrow." Her feelings were conflicting as she got to her feet. There was relief, of course, that now they were out of danger and everything would be taken care of. But there was also dismay at the thought of how her parents would react to the stolen things, to Jerry and Mark being there, to the mess the house had gotten into. And there was even a trace of disappointment, which she didn't understand but had no time to wonder at. She hurried to the window.

"But it's not them!" she said, turning briefly to Jerry, then back to the window. "It's a man, and he's stopping here."

"*The* man?" said Jerry, getting to his feet.

"Of course not. Who could it be?"

"You mean it's not your parents?" said Mark, who had come quietly into the room.

"No." She turned to them. "But who could it be? What if it's somebody my parents asked to check on me? And then he'll see you guys here."

"Do you want us to hide?" Jerry said quickly.

"Oh, I don't know. It seems so silly. If only I knew who he was!"

The doorbell rang.

"Wait in here," she said. "I'll go see who it is." She hurried through the living room and swung open the door.

The first thing that occurred to her was that she knew she'd seen him before. He was an over-large man with a big belly, big clumsy hands, and a big wrinkled nose. He was wearing an orange poncho.

"Mom or Dad home, miss?" he said in a rather grating voice with the local accent. "I'm Inspector Thompson, from the Marsh Harbor police."

"Oh," she said, "the police. Oh."

Now she knew where she had seen him; he was the man who had bumped into her at the herring run, who had been so frantic to get his net into the water that he hadn't even noticed he had practically knocked her down. She remembered how infuriated she had been.

"Well? Are they home?" he repeated.

"Oh. No, they aren't, but — "

"When'll they be back?"

"Tomorrow. They're coming back tomorrow." The police! What a wonderful coincidence. Now she wouldn't even have to go to the store. She could just tell him, and he'd take her away someplace safe, and Jerry and Mark could leave, and the police would guard the house. It couldn't be more perfect.

"So you're all alone out here? A little girl like you?"

"Well, not exactly." The memory of her irritation returned. She didn't like being called a little girl, and suddenly she wondered what his attitude would be about Jerry and Mark. But once she told him what was happening, he couldn't possibly think it was wrong for them to be there. "Some, um . . . friends of mine are staying here too," she went on. "Um, maybe you should come in."

The inspector made the room seem smaller than it was. When he saw Mark and Jerry, standing awkwardly by the fireplace, his eyes narrowed. "Boys!" he said. "These boys are staying here with you?" He looked back and forth from the boys to Lillian. "Say," he said slowly, "do your folks know about this?"

Mark was staring at the inspector as if he were a slug that had just crawled up his leg. Jerry was trying to look pleasant, smiling at the man, but Lillian knew him well enough by now to tell that that last remark had made him uncomfortable. She looked down modestly, then beamed up at the inspector, showing her dimples.

"Well, not really," she said, her hands behind her back. "Jerry and Mark were on a bike trip. It started to rain, and they had no place to stay. My parents would have done the same thing."

Mark made an artificial cough, as if to say she shouldn't have told the inspector the truth. But if he was going to help them, she felt, she had to tell him everything.

"Yeah, but if they'd done the same thing, they would have been here," the inspector said brilliantly. "And they're not here. And I'll bet they wouldn't like their little girl inviting boys in to stay. You better watch it, miss, there're some real weirdos around these days."

"Oh, I know," said Lillian. "In fact, it's lucky you —"

He turned to face the boys. "And you guys better be careful too. Do you know what you're getting into? Sure, it's just dandy to get a free place to sleep with a girl thrown in" (Lillian felt indignant at this), "but she's underage, you know. You can get in serious trouble that way."

"We're underage too," said Mark.

"No wisecracks now. I can see that. You'd be in a real bad way if she should start to kick up a fuss, or if her folks found out and didn't like it."

"But it isn't like that," said Lillian. "We're just friends. And anyway, there's something —"

"What's your name?" he said, whipping out a pen and notebook.

"Please listen," Lillian said. "There's this —"

"Just your name, miss."

Lillian sighed, and gave him her name, her parents' names, and their address in the city. Then Jerry, and Mark, reluctantly, gave him theirs. The inspector studied what he had written for a moment, then snapped the book shut.

"Now listen," he said, "I don't know what's going on here, but I'm not sure I like it. Boys and girls your age, staying together by yourselves in a house like this, it's not right. We don't like that kinda thing around here, and your folks are going to find out about it."

"I was going to tell them anyway," said Lillian, beginning to sound slightly hostile, "and I know they won't care."

"All the worse for them," said the inspector. "People come from the city, think they can do anything out here. Well, we don't like it. I know what goes on with you city kids, I read the paper. And by the way," he said slowly, studying Jerry's hair with distaste, "you guys got any drugs on you? Any pot?"

"Oh, no," said Jerry quickly. "Really, we don't. We don't have anything."

"Yeah," the inspector said, looking for the first time around the room, as if Jerry's words were hardly worth listening to. His gaze rested on the table, the dirty dishes and dried-up food, on the floor around the fireplace, littered with wood chips and ashes, on Lillian's brush and comb, the damp towels, ponchos, shoes and socks that were strewn around the room, on the rumpled rug and disorderly chairs. "Yeah," he repeated, "maybe you do and maybe you don't. But as far as I'm concerned, I wouldn't put it past anybody living in this pigpen. These summer people. . . ." He looked at his watch. "But whatever the hell goes on here, I don't have the time now to find out. I'm busy. There've been some robberies in the area. That's what I came to tell you about. The summer people go away and leave their houses full of expensive things, and then other people come from the city and take them. And I have to take care of it. But I know who's doing it. Know who it is?" he said, pointing at Lillian.

"Who?"

"I know," the inspector went on. "Dope addicts. They come out here and steal to feed their lousy habit. They take dope instead of working and then live off people who work for a living."

"But," Mark burst out, "it's not always like that. One of our teachers was telling us, a lot of people can't get jobs, and they have to live in tenements, and they take drugs because their lives are so miserable, and they get addicted, but they don't have any money, so — "

"Oh, don't give me that," said the inspector. "I grew up in a family with nine kids. My father was dead. My mother worked hard to bring us up decently. None of us had to take drugs. We worked! We didn't have time for ugly habits."

"But a lot of people can't get jobs now."

"Listen, if people want to work, they can get work. Believe me, I know what I'm talking about. But people don't want to work anymore. And then the taxpayers are supposed to support them."

"But," Mark said helplessly, looking at Jerry and Lillian. She wished he would shut up, but she remembered what Jerry had said about how Mark could never stop himself when he felt he was right. "But our teacher said the government should have clinics to try to help them," he went on, "and figure out ways to cure them. Then they wouldn't have to steal anymore."

"There's only one way to get off that stuff, and that's cold turkey. You know what that is? You just stop. That's all, you just stop. It's possible. I stopped smoking cigarettes. But none of these guys have the guts for that. And what are you on their side for, anyway? Do you take drugs?"

"No," said Mark tiredly.

"Well, I've got to get going," said the inspector. "But I'm telling you, there're weirdos in this area, sneaking around and stealing things. People have been missing things, and strangers have been seen in the woods. They're probably addicts and probably dangerous. So watch out. Have you seen anything?"

Mark looked back and forth between Jerry and Lillian. They were staring at each other. Jerry's face was blank, and Lillian forced hers into the same expression. She opened her mouth, then closed it.

"Well?" said the inspector. "What's the matter?"

"I'm just thinking," said Lillian sharply. She looked at Mark for an instant. It was crazy, but all at once she saw the man, not as the demented face behind the woodpile or the sinister figure in her room, but as the lonely and frightened outcast that Mark had described. It would be an outrage for her to turn him in to this odious man who treated them like babies and idiots and wouldn't listen to a word they said. She turned back to Jerry, trying to tell him with her eyes not to say anything. "I'm trying to remember if I saw anything," she went on. "I don't *think* so. Did you guys see anyone?"

Mark's cheeks were glowing, as they always did in moments of crisis. He was staring at her as though he couldn't believe what she had just done, as though she were an entirely different person.

"No," Jerry was saying, "I don't think so."

"Well, watch out. And call the operator if you

see anything strange. And I don't like it, but I guess you boys ought to stay here with her until her folks get back. They getting back soon?"

"I told you they were coming back tomorrow."

"Tell them to get in touch with me when they do. I want to tell them about it myself." He glanced around the room preparing to leave. "Where's the phone?" he said. "I want to call in to headquarters."

"Oh," said Lillian. "Um, well, the phone, it's, I mean —"

"It's not down here?"

"Uh, no."

"Oh, well, forget it. I'll be back there in a few minutes anyway. Now you kids be careful. Remember what I said. I'd send you boys on your way if it weren't for this business. Lock your doors," he added, as he started across the room. Lillian hurried after him.

"You sure you can take care of yourself with those two boys? You really trust them?" he said to her at the door.

"Of course. They're old friends. Their parents are friends of my parents."

"Well, all right," he said. "These kids. . . ." The door slammed.

Lillian came back into the cozy room and collapsed into a chair.

"Lillian," Mark said, "you didn't tell him. Even after what happened to you last night, you didn't tell him."

Lillian still didn't quite understand what she had done; its implications were slowly unraveling back into her mind. Here she was, putting herself in danger for the sake of someone else whom she didn't even know, for the sake of the very person who was creating the danger. She felt like a heroine, like Joan of Arc or somebody. It was a marvelous, heady sensation, much nicer than the few moments of euphoria she had felt from the wine.

"I couldn't stand to when it came right down to it," she said to Mark, a smile hovering around her lips. "I was going to, but after those things he said, I just didn't want to tell him anything. I couldn't stand to be on his side. Oh, it was stupid, I know. Now what's going to happen to us? That was our last chance. But you know," she continued thoughtfully, trying to piece together all the impossible events that led to her decision, "that man last night, he could have hurt me, and he didn't. And that inspector made me feel that what you said about not telling the police could be right, Mark."

Jerry was grinning, obviously so pleased and relieved at the blooming rapport between Lillian and Mark that he had forgotten, for the moment, to be frightened by their situation. He put his hand on Mark's shoulder. "Good old Mark," he said. "He may seem crazy sometimes, but I guess he usually has the right idea."

"I'm begining to realize that," said Lillian, now openly smiling at Mark. He smiled back at her. He had never smiled at her before.

Fifteen

Mark may have had the right idea, and there had certainly been something wickedly daring in not telling the inspector about their predicament — especially because of the way she and Jerry had made the same decision at the last moment simply by looking at each other. But now, in the darkening afternoon, faced with the same situation (except that they were, perhaps, even more helpless now), the euphoric feeling of noble sacrifice was fading quickly, and what they were doing began to seem to Lillian like some pointless game, with unknown risks.

Jerry sighed, and jostled a log with the poker. The wood was so wet that the fire barely did more than glow fitfully and produce a lot of sizzling and smoke. "I wish this fire was better," he said, not trying to hide the whine in his voice.

"I wish everything wasn't such a mess," said Lillian, scraping a twig along the hearth.

"I wish it would stop raining," said Mark from

the table, where he sat staring out into the wet twilight.

"You haven't seen anything outside, have you?" Lillian asked.

"Only this lousy rain."

Lillian threw the twig into the fire. "I'm sure my parents have been trying to call," she said, "I wonder what they think has happened? Maybe they'll come back. . . ."

"And Hugo," Jerry said. "We've *got* to call him, I mean, they'll think something happened to us, and they'll call our folks, and they'll be worried. When we do get back, they'll be so furious they'll never let us go away again."

"Why don't you go to the store and call him, then?" said Mark, still staring out the window.

"But it's so far, isn't it? And it's raining and everything. You don't mind the rain, Mark, you like to ride more than me."

"Hugo's your friend, and I went to the store last time."

"But Mark." Jerry was rocking slightly, his hands pressed between his knees. He was getting so nervous that he even let himself sound irritated. "You ripped out the phone, after all. If you hadn't done it, we could call from here."

"Oh, big deal," said Lillian. "You guys don't have anything to worry about. Your parents aren't the ones whose TV and radio got stolen and whose phone got ripped out. And when you tell them what happened, they'll think you were right to stay. My parents are really going to go insane. But it's funny, I keep forgetting about it. I mean, everything is like a dream. What are we doing? It's like we're just sitting here, waiting for something. But what? And we keep getting farther and farther away from the world, from everything except each other, and this house, and . . . that man."

"I wonder if he'll come back," Jerry said.

Lillian wondered too. The fire crackled and hissed. Is that what we're waiting for? she asked herself. And who was he? Her mind kept swinging back and forth. At first he had been terrifying, almost a monster, when she had seen him behind the woodpile and when he had come into her room. But afterward something had changed, probably because he hadn't hurt her, and when she was faced with the inspector, the man outside had become hunted and sad, struggling pitifully in a hostile world. And now her mind had changed again. She thought of the missing things, and the man seemed cold and dangerous, unpredictable, a silent shadow who watched them, unseen, with plans they did not know.

"I wonder if we did the right thing," Jerry said.

"Nobody stopped you from telling him," said Mark.

"Why do you keep being so mean?" Jerry asked. "I wanted to tell him, but I could tell nobody wanted me to, so I didn't. Now I wish I had."

"I'm not being mean, I just wish you'd stop talking about it; what's done is done." Mark stood up, and it occurred to Lillian that he too might be having second thoughts. It bothered her, for it made her question what they had done even more. "And you could always go and call that inspector yourself, you know," Mark added.

"I know," said Jerry, "I *know*. Could you turn on the light?"

"Then we won't be able to see anything outside," said Lillian.

"So? What difference would it make? The doors are already locked."

"There's nothing to see outside but rain," said Mark. "And I'm sick of looking at it." He stretched, and walked over to the light switch on the wall. There was a brief flash, and then darkness again.

"Oh, now what?" cried Lillian.

"The bulb must have burned out." Mark flipped the switch several times. Nothing happened.

Lillian climbed reluctantly to her feet. "Now I suppose I have to change the bulb. Mark, you take the lantern down and I'll go look for a bulb."

She couldn't find one. She had never paid much attention to where things were kept in the house, for whenever something like a light bulb or an extension cord was needed her parents leapt to get it themselves. She returned to the cozy room to find Mark still struggling with the lantern and Jerry watching him apprehensively.

"Hey!" said Lillian, "Stop. I can't find a — "

"What?" said Mark, turning toward her sharply.

There was a sudden clatter of dishes as the lantern hit the tabletop. Mark grabbed for it, but not in time to keep it from rolling off into a burst of glass on the floor.

"Oh, *no*!" Lillian cried from the doorway. In

an instant she was crouching over the smashed lantern, which was now nothing but a frame with a few shards of glass clinging to it.

Mark was still standing on the chair. "Oh, what have I done now?" he said awkwardly. "I'm sorry, Lillian. It was heavy, and it just sort of slipped — "

"Oh, stop it!" she said. "This is the worst thing that could ever happen! They loved this stupid thing."

"Maybe . . . we could get it fixed," Jerry said.

"Oh, we cannot," Lillian moaned. "Don't be silly. And the phone, and the TV, and this horrible mess! The whole house is completely falling apart. My parents, they're going to . . . I just can't . . . and I couldn't even find a bulb." She sat down on the floor and buried her head in her hands.

Mark climbed down from the chair as quietly as possible and sat next to Jerry. They stared solemnly into the fire while Lillian sat silently behind them, just beyond the range of its feeble glow.

At last Lillian looked up. "Oh well," she said, and came over to the fire on her knees, pushing her way in between them, "I guess it doesn't matter. Everything else is so crazy, that lamp will hardly make any difference. Anyway, my parents will probably be so relieved that I'm alive that they won't be able to stay angry very long. If I am alive."

Twilight had faded, and behind them the room was full of shadows. In the darkness the sound of the rain was closer, and the wind, and the distant gulls. It was an unbearably cold and wet and lonely sound. But beside Lillian was Jerry's solemn face, and Mark's impassive one, warm in the firelight. And it occurred to her then how much better it was to be inside, with a fire and friends, than outside and alone.

"Every time I hear that sound I can't help seeing the herring," Mark said. "When are those gulls going to stop?"

"It can't go on much longer," said Lillian. She looked behind her for a moment. "I guess we're just going to have to stay in the dark, unless we want to go into another room and freeze."

"Maybe I can build up the fire." Mark poked the embers and laid on more twigs and logs. The wood was drier, the fire began to burn more cheerfully, and the shadows retreated a little farther behind them.

Still, there was no doubt about it, Lillian would have felt better if there had been more light. They could have turned on the kitchen and living room lights and left the doors open, but then what little warmth there was would vanish. And the three of them seemed to be enveloped in a strange lethargy — no one even moved to pick up the broken glass or bring in a lamp from another room. At least the darkness made the depressing mess around them less apparent.

They sat, not speaking, as the evening grew into night. Staring at the flames, Lillian felt her other senses grow sharper. She began to notice the smell of old food from the kitchen; she listened to the creaking of the house in the wind, and tried to convince herself that it was not footsteps. Occasionally she felt the touch of cold air on her neck, and wondered if perhaps a window, or a door, had been left open. She knew that something had to break the spell they were under, that someone had to move, or decide what they should do. But it could not be her. The thought of leaving the fire and going into the darkness, even to turn on a light, filled her with the nameless but intense terror of a child alone at night. The very air around them seemed to crackle with anticipation, to press down on her, until she felt that she could not even turn her head for fear of what might be behind her. Tense, but unable to move, she waited, and the sound of her heartbeat seemed to fill the room.

And then there was a crash, and the spell was broken.

Sixteen

"What was that?" Lillian shrieked.

All at once the three of them were standing. Lillian felt her fingers tightening on Mark's elbow. "Where did it come from?"

"Somewhere over there," said Mark. "But it didn't sound like it was in the kitchen." He broke away from her and stepped to the kitchen door. Slowly he pushed it open a crack and looked through. "There's no one there."

"It sounded like it was beyond the kitchen, but inside," Jerry said.

Mark was already through the kitchen door, moving quietly. Lillian and Jerry slipped in behind him. It was cold in the room; the smooth, hard floor bit into Lillian's bare feet. There was a thick, garbagey smell that she had never noticed when her mother was there.

"Maybe it came from the storeroom by the back door," Mark whispered. "Where the bikes are."

"Don't!" Lillian grabbed his arm as he moved away, but he shook her off and stepped into the little entryway beside the kitchen. They could see him peering into the storeroom beyond, where the bikes glinted dully.

There was another noise, like something heavy dropping onto a wood floor.

"Lillian!" Mark hissed, beckoning. "Is there another room? It seemed to come through the wall here."

"The toolshed! It's connected to the house, but you can't get there from inside. Oh, no," she moaned. "My father's tools."

"But how do you get to it?" demanded Mark.

"There's a door outside. In the backyard. To the right of the porch. But —"

Mark slipped the chain loose, clicked the lock, and carefully pulled open the door. The sound of the rain blew in at them, along with a chill dampness. Mark stepped out on the porch. Lillian, unable to resist, peered over his shoulder. Jerry stood nervously in the doorway.

The small wing of the house, with a lower roof, was several yards from where they stood. Its door hung open, and out of it came hurried noises and a darting beam of light.

"My father's tools," Lillian whispered frantically. "He's stealing my father's tools."

"He must have thought we were gone because of the light being off," said Mark.

Lillian's terror suddenly drained away, replaced by self-righteous fury. "But," she said, her voice rising, "we just saved him! How can he do this to us, after we just saved him?"

"Oh, be quiet," Jerry whispered. "He'll hear you. And how could he possibly know what we did?"

"And you!" she said to Mark, backing away from him. "It's your fault, it's all your fault. We didn't tell because of you. Everything we did to save him was because of you. And look what happens! He just keeps coming back and taking more and more."

"Shhh!" said Mark, his face in the darkness twisting into a worried frown. "He might have a — "

"Oh, I don't care!" She stepped off the porch, still staring at him. The grass was cold and wet. "We've got to stop him. He can't take my father's things!"

And then the beam of light swung into her eyes, and she couldn't see. She heard Jerry gasp from the porch. She moved her head frantically back and forth, but the light stayed in her eyes until she spun around and closed them. She turned back to find Jerry and Mark, transfixed, watching a dark figure with an electric saw under one arm run toward the woods.

"No!" Lillian screamed hoarsely, starting after him. "Stop! Come back! We'll tell the police. They know about you. We'll describe you to them." The man had reached the trees. He kept running, faster than she could. "Oh, please stop! Bring it back, you . . . you rat! They'll catch you. I'll make things up that you did, and they'll believe me! STOP!"

Her last word was a sobbing wail. She could barely see him now. She slowed for a few steps, and then stood still on the edge of the lawn and gave way to her tears. Her hair was plastered to her head and her back; her T-shirt was drenched. She stared sobbing up into the rain, her chin jerking helplessly, as the water coursed down her cheeks.

After what seemed to her like quite a long time, she felt Jerry's arm on her shoulder. "Come on, Lillian," he said softly, "it's not that bad."

"He's right," Mark said gently. "Come on, let's go inside."

"Yes, it is that bad," she gasped between sobs. She thought of how she had betrayed her parents. They had trusted her, and she had done the wrong thing every time, and the house was a shambles. Everything was worse than they ever could have imagined. Her whole life was different now, different and ruined. She could not think of one hopeful thing. With Mark and Jerry on either side of her, she began walking slowly toward the house, utterly defeated.

And then there was a rustle behind them.

Instantly they turned toward the sound. He was standing under the closest trees, not ten feet away from them. In one hand he held the flashlight, in the other arm he clutched her father's electric saw. He was dressed in black, and difficult to see in the darkness except for his face, long and pale. "Could we go inside, out of the rain?" he said.

Seventeen

Lillian couldn't take her eyes from the man's face. In the darkness and rain it was difficult to tell what it was, but it seemed to her that there was something very strange about his face that she hadn't noticed before, something that made her uneasy.

The man's question had been answered only by a stunned silence. "I won't hurt you," he went on, haltingly. "Believe me, I won't. I just want to talk to you. And . . . and you can have the saw. I don't want it after all."

Still no one spoke, or made a move. Lillian turned briefly to Mark, who was also staring intensely at the man's face, as if he were trying to tell whether or not he could believe him.

"Well, then, I'll just put it back," the man said. He stepped into the toolshed. The three of them looked at each other.

"I think . . . maybe we should ask him in," Mark whispered.

"What?" said Jerry. "But, Mark, then he could do anything! Why do you always want to do — "

"I'm going to," Lillian said suddenly, twisting her hands and sniffing. "It's the one chance I have to maybe . . . maybe fix things up a little. My parents wouldn't want me to, and I'm scared to, but maybe we could talk to him and get him to return the — "

He came out of the shed, pushing the door closed and nervously trying to fit together the ruined lock. Lillian stepped forward, pushing away Jerry's restraining hand. "Okay," she said loudly, "you can come in. But — but you better not try anything. The police are looking for you. If anything funny happens, they would know."

"I assure you, I mean no harm," he said, spreading his arms. "It's three to one, and I don't have a gun."

Lillian turned and walked quickly into the house, not looking behind. Jerry and Mark followed, and the man after them. Inside, he stopped to lock the door and slip in the chain. Why should he do that? Lillian wondered, turning to watch. Is someone following him?

The fire, weak to begin with, was almost dead. The open doors had filled the room with cold air, and suddenly Lillian noticed that she was soaking wet, and shivering. Mark squatted to fix the fire while the others stood awkwardly, not saying a word. In the dark room the man's face could still hardly be seen.

Lillian found a large pile of clean towels in the bathroom and brought them over to the fire, looking toward the man but not really at him. "Maybe we should dry off with these," she said.

"That's very kind of you," said the man.

Clustering around the fire, the boys began to remove their shirts. The man's head was turned away, but Lillian watched him to see what she could of him in the firelight. He pulled the black jersey over his head, and Lillian quickly turned away as an icy pang shot from her stomach to her knees. It was not his incredible emaciation, like someone from a concentration camp, that was so terrible, but the way his body was shaking. The nervous twitching of the skin across his ribs and down to his abdomen could not be due just to the cold, it seemed to her, but must come from some deep sickness. It was like the way an old person shakes.

With towels wrapped around their shoulders, the boys arranged their shirts on the hearth and sat down. Lillian saw the man's face sharply for the first time; he wasn't old. He just looks like a guy in college, she thought for an instant. And yet there was a deadness to his face, an absence of expression except for the tension in his mouth, that made her think again of an old person. An old person who was about to die.

She turned away, busily wrapping a towel around her hair. No one seemed to know what to say. The three of them kept glancing intermittently at the man's face, but he only stared blankly into the fire. Lillian, who was sitting beside him, began to feel more and more nervous. The man was behaving so strangely, maybe he really *was* crazy after all. She wondered if they should have asked him in, and found herself wishing that they hadn't, and looked back with longing on the time when they had been without his alien presence. And the man kept shaking, long after they had stopped, a shaking that came from deep inside him, while his face remained blank. The terrible shaking was the most frightening thing of all.

"Didn't you want to say something to us?" Mark said at last.

"What?" the man said, as if he were being awakened. "Oh. Yes, I wanted to talk to you. It's just that it's been so long since I sat by a fire like this. I . . . sort of forgot where I was."

Lillian could feel the others begin to relax, as she did. Somehow, it seemed that a desperate criminal wouldn't say that about a fire.

"It was you who took the radio and TV," she said. "Wasn't it? And you did come into my room last night, I know it was you."

"Yes, it was me," he said softly. "And it was me who scared you from behind the woodpile too. That was what made me come to your room. I couldn't get that expression on your face and the sound of your screaming out of my mind, and I kept thinking, 'What have I become, that I would do that to a little girl — '" He stopped suddenly and looked back into the fire. "But of course that was ridiculous. Why should it bother me just to frighten you, when I've ripped off poor people and sweet little old ladies and double-crossed my friends. . . ."

His voice trailed off as he sank back into thought again. But what could that mean? Lillian wondered. Why did he do all those things? He didn't talk like a criminal, he didn't look like one. Slowly an idea was beginning to take shape in her mind, an answer, something someone had been saying. . . .

"You're an addict, aren't you?" said Mark.

"Yes," said the man, nodding slowly at the fire. "A real-life, hundred-fifty-dollar-a-day junkie. Right before your very eyes."

"You mean you take dope all the time?" Lillian asked tentatively.

"No, I take lemonade!" he said with sudden violence. "What the hell do you *think* I take?"

Lillian turned her head quickly away from him, as if she had been slapped. Jerry, she noticed, was cringing on the other side of Mark. "Yes," the man went on softly again, "I take heroin, and it's beginning to wear off, so I'm getting nasty, and I'm sorry. Why should I expect you to know anything about it, anyway?" He sighed.

"Oh, I do know something about it," Lillian said, trying to make up for the *faux pas* she seemed to have made. "I mean, a lot of kids take pot, and then, if you're real poor, and live in a tenement, and your life is real miserable and everything, and you can't get a job, then it's just natural you would — "

Her voice stuck in her throat. The man was laughing again like he had the other night, so humorlessly that it was painful and frightening to hear. She wanted to put her hands over her ears. Jerry and Mark were staring down at the floor, unable to look at the man now.

"Charming," the man said, pausing to laugh briefly again. "How very liberal of you. However, I don't want to disappoint you, but I'm not one of your inner-city cases. My parents, you will be shocked to hear, are quite well-off. They treated me nicely, gave me everything, sent me to college; I had lots of friends. It was lovely."

"But then why — " Mark said. Oh, don't ask him! Lillian begged silently, not wanting anyone to provoke him again, feeling the whole side of her body tingle with its nearness to this strange man who could change so quickly, and who at any moment might reach out and grab her. She moved slightly, trying to get as far away from him as possible. If only she hadn't asked him in!

"Why did I start? Why not? It was so much fun. It felt marvelous, and it was so terribly illegal, and best of all, I couldn't think of anything my parents would hate more."

"What . . . what did it feel like?" Lillian couldn't keep from asking, feeling a spark of connection to his words.

"Like . . . there was nothing like it. You just felt all warm and happy and relaxed, and everything was beautiful and very funny, and nothing mattered, nothing mattered at all." He was facing them now, gesturing with his hand.

"Did you have hallucinations?" said Jerry, speaking to the man for the first time.

"No, no, none of that psychedelic crap. You just felt good. And nothing mattered, that was the best part."

"But didn't you know you'd get addicted?" Mark asked, frowning.

"Yes, yes, I suppose so." He turned away again. "But I didn't really believe it would happen to me, I didn't know it would be like this.

It was just something to do. And it made me feel like a daring outlaw, like I belonged to this secret forbidden group outside of society. . . . But why am I spouting all this garbage to you?" he said suddenly. "I don't need to confess, especially to — How old are you kids?"

"They're fourteen and I'm fifteen," said Lillian, adjusting the towel on her head. It was weird the way he kept changing so quickly. Sometimes he seemed as if he were about to go to asleep; other times he was irritable, as though the slightest remark could make him angry; and always there was that bitter, oddly humorous sarcasm. Nevertheless, she was beginning to feel more relaxed, and she could sense that the boys were too. He spoke like someone they might know, and there no longer seemed to be much chance that he would kill them, or even steal anything else.

'But didn't you say you wanted to talk to us?" Mark was saying. He was obviously fascinated by the man, leaning forward and watching him intently.

"Did I?" He had lapsed into abstractedness again. In the firelight, the sharp bones and shadows of his face gave him an almost satanic appearance. Mark's round, smooth features were positively angelic in comparison.

"Yes," Mark pressed him. "You did." Jerry shifted uncomfortably in the shadows, looking away for a moment.

The man sighed. "Oh, just what I said before, not to be afraid." He seemed to hate admitting to any feelings of gentleness or compassion. "And . . . you were so upset," he said to Lillian.

"I was sneakier the other times, I never *saw* the effect I could have. It positively wrung my rotten heart. And it was cold as hell out there," he added quickly.

"But — " said Mark. Oh, leave him alone, thought Lillian. Mark could be so irritating, the way he wouldn't let certain subjects drop. Lillian nudged him with her elbow to try to make him stop, but he wouldn't. "But if your parents have money, then how come you have to steal and everything?"

The man stared at him for a moment, his mouth a hard line, as if he couldn't believe Mark had asked him that question. "Man, do you have any idea what it's like to have to come up with a hundred and fifty dollars a day?" he said. "Figure it out, that's over a thousand bucks a week. Even if I were living off my parents, which I don't happen to be, what they could come up with wouldn't make a dent. And don't tell me to get a job. Even if there were any around, I couldn't make more than about three hundred at the most, and I'd be wasting all the time I had to get more. Even what I've taken from here is kind of useless. What I should be doing is going with this guy I know who has a truck; we'd pull up to a place like this when nobody was home and clean it out, take everything in the place — rugs, furniture, dishes, everything. But that was a real hassle, he was such a bastard. And then every once in a while I think about what I'm doing it for, not because it's even fun to turn on or because it makes me feel good, but because if I don't get high, if I don't get high, it's. . . . There's no way to tell you what it's like if I don't get it when I need it, even for a few hours. Like nothing on earth."

"I know you get sick and everything if you stop taking it," Mark went on, "but if you really wanted to, don't they have ways of helping you?"

"They?" he said, "Who is 'they'? Those treatment centers are packed, there's not enough methadone or other crap to go around. And anyway, they're the best places to score."

"But then," Mark continued. Oh, shut *up*! Lillian screamed inside her head. "But then, what can you do? There's nothing you can do. It's completely . . . it sounds completely impossible."

"Just keep doing what I am doing." His voice had a tense, hopeless edge to it. "And I can even rip people off without feeling guilty and going back to explain. I won't keep on feeling guilty much longer, that's for sure. But it was your face, your goddamn frightened face that made me come back, stupidly, when they'd probably be watching the house. God knows why they weren't, God knows why I came back again to the same place. The dumbest thing. And I couldn't even keep running away when I heard your goddamn crying. Jesus, I must *want* to get caught." He closed his eyes and began rubbing them, slowly but nervously.

Lillian was sitting up, her eyes glistening. Why, Mark had been right all along! The man was helpless, a victim. He wasn't insane, he wasn't *really* a criminal, he didn't mean anyone any harm. "And guess what?" she said to him.

"You want to hear something? We didn't even call the police, we didn't do anything. We were going to, but Mark pulled out the phone. He said it wasn't fair." The man slowly looked up at her. "And then a policeman came to the house, and we didn't even tell him anything was gone, we didn't tell him that I saw you, or anything."

"But why the hell *not*?"

"Because of Mark," Lillian said, beaming proudly and gesturing toward him. "Because Mark kept saying we didn't really know, and it might not be fair." She had forgotten completely about asking the man if he still had the radio and the TV, which was the reason she had invited him in.

"You're crazy," the man said, looking at Mark.

"I . . . ," said Mark.

"But he saved you!" Lillian cried, "And you say he's crazy?"

"Yes, but he couldn't have known it was me. It might have been a real criminal. You might have all been killed!"

Lillian groaned in frustration. "It *was* sort of crazy," said Mark with difficulty. "But I couldn't help it. I don't like the police, I didn't want to turn them on somebody, and especially somebody. . . ." He was struggling to get the words out. ". . . somebody who was alone. I — I'm alone a lot. I'm always on the side of somebody who's alone, that's all. It seemed like we'd be hurting you more than you could hurt us, or something," he finished lamely.

No one spoke for a moment, as the man stared at him in disbelief. "But what about me?" Jerry said suddenly. "You're not alone when you're with me."

"I know," said Mark, "but . . . I don't know . . . I guess I always thought you would just be with me when you couldn't be with the other kids, that you didn't really . . . oh, forget it!" Even in the firelight, Lillian could see that he was blushing.

"But Jerry likes you better than anyone, I know he does, Mark," she said. She didn't know how she knew, but she knew.

"Yes," Jerry said, practically whispering, "I do."

"That's amazing," the man said, shaking his head, "Amazing! A kid your age, thinking that way. Remarkable. Most adults wouldn't begin to think about someone else in that situation. And you others went along with it." He kept shaking his head. "It's beautiful, kind of stupid and dangerous, but beautiful. And that I should stumble into you kids. You're damn lucky it *was* me, you know. Anybody else, and you'd be. . . ." He didn't finish.

"Well, Mark always takes care of wounded animals." Jerry said lightly, once again trying to make Mark, who seemed embarrassed, feel more comfortable.

"And he couldn't stop *thinking* about the herring and the gulls," said Lillian. "It never occurred to me to think about them at all."

"Oh yeah, those goddamn gulls were driving me crazy out there with their lousy screeching. It was all I needed, waiting out there in the rain."

"Oh, so you *were* waiting out there. We were

wondering about how you knew when — " Jerry began. And then, in an instant, they were all on their feet.

"Cars, a whole lot of cars!" Lillian screamed from the window, as the headlight beams raced across the ceiling and walls, and the sound of motors and squealing brakes blotted out the rain.

Eighteen

"Run!" Mark shouted.

Dropping his towel, the man stood looking wildly around him, his ribs standing out in the firelight, his eyes wide and unreal and still strangely expressionless.

"Run!" Mark shouted again, thrusting the man's shirt against his shaking chest. "They're coming inside!"

Mark and Lillian began pushing him toward the back door, with Jerry hovering behind, as the man struggled to get into his still damp shirt. They were fumbling with the chain and the lock, slowing each other down, when the banging on the front door began.

"Let me!" the man said, pushing their hands away, and pulled open the door. "Good-bye," he said, turning to them on the porch and suddenly whispering. "You kids, you're beautiful. Thanks."

There was the sound of splintering wood, and heavy footsteps in the front hall. "Those rats!"

Lillian screamed, darting toward the noise, as Mark quietly shut and locked the door.

It was the inspector, of course, with five men behind him, none of them in uniform, suddenly filling the living room. They were all out of breath, and their eyes darted about them as they stood with their arms held tensely at their sides. Two of them had rifles, and the inspector had a small gun.

For a moment all Lillian could do was stare in terrified fascination at the guns. She had never seen a gun before, and they looked suprisingly unreal. Then she realized what was happening. "What are you doing here?" she screamed at them, her hands clenched and her towel turban slowly unwinding itself. "Why did you have to break open the door? Who told you to come here? Who said you could come in?"

Ignoring her, the inspector gestured toward the stairway. "You two, look up there," he said, and two of the men tramped nosily up the stairs.

Mark had come quietly up behind her, and suddenly she remembered that neither of the boys was wearing a shirt. "What are you *doing* here?" she screamed again. "It's my house, and I order you to leave!" Outside the window she could see moving shapes with flashlights; she heard dogs barking and harsh voices shouting and even some raucous laughter. It sounded like a hunting party.

"Cut the hysterics," said the inspector, sounding like a bad television detective. "We know he's here. The sooner we find him, the better it'll be for all of you."

"Who's here?" Lillian said. "What are you talking about?" Lying to these men seemed so necessary and right to her that she didn't even have to think about what to say.

"You know who I mean." The inspector was beginning to shout as well. The other men were shuffling their feet, still panting; ready for action, they seemed to be unprepared for this delay. "One of your dope fiends from the city. He was being followed —"

There was a sharp intake of breath from Mark. The inspector turned on him. "Yes, followed. We know he came into the house, and that you kids let him in. So now tell me where the hell he is and —"

Outside, the shouting rose suddenly in pitch, almost to a shrieking; there were snarls, and then a quick barrage of explosions.

"What was *that*?" Lillian cried.

"Outside!" commanded the inspector. They hurried out the front door, followed quickly by the men from upstairs.

"Those noises," Lillian said, her face white, "they sounded like —"

"Shots," Mark finished, starting for the back door. Lillian raced after him, Jerry following behind a little slowly.

From the porch they could make out a cluster of figures down among the trees, silhouetted against a pool of flashlight beams. The inspector and his group were running toward them through the brush. Mark jumped from the porch without hesitation and Lillian followed quickly. Halfway across the lawn she turned back briefly to see what had happened to Jerry. He was still standing on the porch. When he saw her look at him he hurried down the steps after her. He must be afraid, she thought, following Mark into the trees, and for an instant she wondered why she wasn't. It hadn't even occurred to her to think that she might get shot; all that was in her mind was the man, and what these rats were doing to him. She didn't notice the brambles scratching at her legs, the stones on the ground, her wet clothes getting even wetter. She didn't hesitate to shoulder her way roughly into the circle of men.

Then she moaned, involuntarily, as though she were sick. How strange, that the ugly, horrifying part wasn't the holes in the man's head, or the blood soaking onto the ground, but his face. His eyes were open, his mouth still held in a tense line. His whole expression was no different than it had been when he was alive; and that, somehow, was the unbearable part, the part that made her stomach shrink inside her and her knees begin to give way.

Mark was standing beside her, his face an odd shade of yellow in a stray flashlight beam. He reached out to steady her, then, seeing her face, pushed her around and began leading her back up the slope. When they reached Jerry, who was standing halfway down from the lawn, she paid no attention to the tall man who looked at her briefly, then hurried past down toward the others. "Come on, Jerry," Mark said. "She needs help."

Jerry took a few quick steps to her side, and he

and Mark helped her up the hill. "The man," Jerry whispered, "Is he . . .?"

"He's dead," Mark said.

"I think I'm going to be sick to my stomach," Lillian said. "My knees aren't even there at all, they don't work. Don't hate me if I throw up. I think I'm going to."

"Put your head between your knees," Mark said as they eased her into a chair at the table, and she stayed that way as they sat down. She couldn't tell how long they sat there in the dark room, not speaking, hearing the rustling and the murmuring voices from outside, hearing the familiar sounds of the rain, and, faintly, the gulls. Once again, she couldn't get the man's face out of her mind, but this time it was so much worse. What she saw was uglier, and, though she didn't understand just what it meant, this time there was no hope.

Finally she heard footsteps in the kitchen, and through her fingers saw the light there go on. Someone came into the room. "Can you tell me what happened here?" a deep voice said matter-of-factly. Lillian lifted her head from her knees. It was a tall man with tightly curling gray hair, the man who had been standing behind Jerry on the hillside. She put her head back on her knees.

"Who are you?" said Mark.

"I'm the chief of police."

"Then what is there to tell?" Mark's voice was expressionless, as though he were trying not to betray any emotion. "He was a criminal. You killed him. Isn't that all that matters to you?"

"Look," the man said, "most of those men out

there are not on the force. And the ones who are won't be for long."

"You mean it was like a . . . a mob, or a lynching, or something?" Jerry asked.

"That's exactly what it was like. And it shouldn't have happened. It could have been prevented. But something went terribly wrong here. I've got to know what it was, so it won't happen again. Now," and unexpectedly, his voice became gentler, "I wish you would tell me how all of you were involved. Out there, they're saying you were harboring him here. Thompson even said he thought you were in on it with him. That's hard for me to believe." He sat down in the other chair at the table, facing them. "You've got to trust me," he finished.

Lillian had raised her head again; Mark was leaning forward, looking closely at the man's face. "Well . . . ," Mark said.

"He seems all right," Lillian said faintly. The man hadn't even noticed the mess. "Not like that other guy." Somehow they seemed to have the right, because of what had happened, to talk openly about the police chief before his face.

"Well, okay," said Mark. "You're not like those other people. I guess it began when — "

"Begin with telling me why you're all here," the police said. "I want to know everything."

And so Lillian and Mark told him, interrupting each other, reinforcing each other, while the chief listened patiently, asking occasional questions; and Jerry sat silent in a kind of isolation, listening to them almost as if it was a story he hadn't heard. It was strange how close Lillian felt to Mark now, as if he were a brother; strange how the involvement they shared, from which Jerry was somehow distant, made Jerry suddenly the outsider.

". . . at first I wasn't sure," she finished. "But after we talked to him and everything, and after . . . what just happened, well, then I just knew that we, I mean Mark, had been right all along, that we had done the right things."

The policeman shifted in his seat. "Hmmm," he said, "I'm not so sure about that. What you did was certainly . . . unusual — "

"I knew it!" Mark interrupted, turning to Lillian. "We shouldn't have trusted him."

"Hold on, hold on," the chief said, waving him down with his hand. "What you did was certainly courageous, and well-intentioned, I suppose. But one thing you forgot is that the police aren't always the enemies of people like him. That boy out there might very well be alive now if you had reported him sooner, before that mob had a chance to get started. What we try to do, some of us, anyway, is to help his kind of person, not destroy them."

No one spoke. The confusion Lillian had felt before the events of the evening suddenly filled her mind again, laced now with guilt and horror. Quickly she looked back and forth between Jerry and Mark, but neither would catch her eye. "But," she said, the confusion growing inside her as though it might explode, "but — "

"I'm not saying it's your fault," the chief said, standing up. "But please, in the future, remember that the law isn't always wrong. Oh, and by the way," he turned to Lillian, "your parents are frantic."

She started. "My parents? I forgot all about them."

"They've been trying and trying to call you, and weren't able to, of course. They finally reached me before I left the station. They'll be here tomorrow."

"My parents," Lillian said, her voice rising. "What am I going to tell them? They'll go crazy when they find out what we did. And the house, and, and everything. They'll never understand, they'll think it was the most insane thing in the world for us to invite him in, and not call the police. They'll never trust me again, they'll watch me like hawks! I forgot all about them. . . ." Her voice trailed off and she let her head sink into her hands.

"I'm afraid there's no way of avoiding it," the chief said. "But I suspect they won't be as angry as you think. And I'd suggest," he added, looking for the first time around the room, "that you clean this place up before they get here. I've got to go now. Remember what I said." Very quickly and quietly he was gone.

Lillian turned to Mark. He was staring straight ahead, his face impassive. "Do you think . . . do you think what he said. . . ?" she asked. Mark did not move or respond. "But what if it *was* our fault?" she shouted.

"No!" Jerry said. "Don't think that. Forget what he said. Don't worry, please, of course it wasn't." He seemed to be talking to Mark more than to her. "That guy was a cop, just like the others, it was just garbage what —"

"No it wasn't," Mark interrupted quietly. "It

was not garbage, Jerry. It was true, now I know it, he was right. It's my fault he's dead."

"No it isn't," Jerry pleaded. "It isn't, Mark. Don't let yourself think that. And anyway, even if he was alive, if we'd reported him, where would he be now? In prison somewhere. And he'd probably just keep on being a dope addict and a criminal. You can't let yourself — "

"Oh shut up, shut up!" Mark shouted, holding his ears and shaking his head. "Stop trying to be so nice! Don't you even realize, don't you even care? Do you think it's better that he's dead? You can't say that. Maybe he would have been cured, maybe they could have helped him."

"But Mark, you're just being morbid," Jerry said. "You always think whatever is difficult or unpleasant is right. Why do you have to worry about everything so much?"

"But maybe we did kill him," Lillian said, wishing she could believe Jerry, trying to, but still unable to discard Mark's words.

"But it wasn't our fault," Jerry insisted. "Can't you see that? We were just trying to do what was right."

"Well," Lillian said thoughtfully, "we were, weren't we? I suppose it would have been different if you weren't here, Mark, we would have just called the police, but then. . . ." She paused, then continued slowly. "But then . . . we never would have met the man, we would never have known that he really was okay, that he wasn't horrible. And maybe we . . . maybe we made him feel good, that we tried to help him."

"Yes," Jerry said, leaning toward Mark. "She's

right, don't you see? You were trying to help him."

"We were just wrong to think we could do it ourselves, I guess," Lillian went on. "If only that inspector hadn't been so horrible, we still might have told the police. In a way it was more the inspector's fault than ours."

Jerry was nodding. "Maybe it was partly our fault, but not as much as his. You were only trying to do what was right, Mark. It was their fault — "

"Those rats!" Lillian put in, beginning to sob.

"Their fault," Jerry continued. "How were we supposed to know they'd kill him? We never imagined anybody would do that. How could we ever know that people could be so terrible?"

"Now I'll know," said Mark.

Nineteen

At first Lillian hardly knew what was happening; the sensation was so unusual that she had almost forgotten what it was like. But when she opened her eyes she knew at once that the warmth in her face was real, for sunshine so bright that it made her squint was streaming through the window. She was out of bed in an instant and stretching her head outside. There wasn't a cloud in the sky, the wind was warm on her face, and there was a strange silence over the marsh. On her way downstairs she realized what it was: the gulls had stopped.

She had no trouble rousing Jerry and Mark; the unexpected sun was like a holiday. Even the mess, which by now had spread itself like an infection from the cozy room throughout most of the house, seemed less formidable in the bright light. Breakfast did not take long, for they were all conscious of how little time they had. They all raced about frantically, hardly speaking, and by lunchtime the house was as close as they could possibly make it to what it had been before.

Sitting at the polished table with peanut butter sandwiches, Jerry and Mark's damp, stuffed packs leaning against the wall in a patch of sunlight, the night before began to seem to Lillian like something from another world. The thought of it still made her stomach turn, and brought a terrible black feeling into her mind; no one she knew had ever died, and the idea that the man simply did not exist anymore, although she knew it was true, was difficult really to believe. But she also found herself thinking about her normal life, and looking forward to it; and even looking forward to seeing her parents.

Mark took it the worst, of course. But after she had explained to him, over and over again, that it really wasn't his fault, he suddenly began to stare at her, his cheeks growing red in that way they had, and said, "You know, Lillian, I believe you." It was slightly awkward for a moment, and she didn't say anything. She had never expected to like him as much as she did.

She tried to persuade them to stay until her parents arrived, but they insisted that they had to leave, and she did not pursue it. Somehow she felt they wouldn't belong in the house with her parents there; Jerry and Mark were part of something that was separate from the rest of her life. And she felt she could handle her parents better on her own.

Standing on the road, the boys holding their bikes, Lillian felt close to them both, and sad that they were going away; but she also wasn't sure that they would ever see each other again. She waved after them many times as they rode off, shouting good-byes, and stood on the road until they were out of sight.

Then Lillian went into the house. She washed the lunch dishes, planning what she would say to her parents. She wandered about inside aimlessly for a while, then found her book and her brush and went out onto the back lawn. She sat in the sun, brushing her hair for quite a long time. When she stopped, she did not pick up her book, but stared, hardly moving, out across the marsh and the water. The gulls, in quiet clusters, soared gracefully in the clear light.

And then she heard the sound of a car stopping by the house, and quick footsteps approaching.

ABOUT THE BOOK

One spring Blair Lent and I were both working in a house by the sea. Blair was finishing a new story for a picture book, and I was looking for a new idea. There was a herring run behind the house, and it was the time of year when the stream was full of fish and the gulls were out in noisy swarms to catch them. We went for a walk on the beach and began making up a complicated story about the place, full of absurd events. There was one idea, however, that began to dominate: the struggle between the gulls and the fish would have its counterpart in the human events of the story. As the walk continued the story became longer and more serious, and by the time we got back to the house we had worked out the whole plot of *Run*, just as, several years earlier, we had worked out the concept and plot of *Blackbriar* together. Then I sat down and began to write.

—WILLIAM SLEATOR